Heavenly Honeymoon

by

Kathi Daley

This book is dedicated to all my fans who love Zoe and Zak as much as I do.

I also want to thank the very talented Jessica Fischer for the cover art.

I so appreciate Bruce Curran, who is always ready and willing to answer my cyber questions.

Special thanks to Joanne Kocourek, Joyce Aiken, Pamela Curran, Vivian Shane, Nancy Farris, and Janel Flynn for their contribution of recipes for *Heavenly Honeymoon*.

And, of course, thanks to the readers and bloggers in my life who make doing what I do possible, especially everyone who hangs out and likes and share my posts at Kathi Daley Books Group Page.

I want to thank Randy Ladenheim-Gil for the editing.

And last but not least, I want to thank my sister Christy who is always willing to pitch in with an opinion when I need one, and a special thank you to my husband Ken, who allows me the time I need to write but taking care of everything else.

Books by Kathi Daley

Come for the murder, stay for the romance.
Buy them on Amazon today.

Zoe Donovan Cozy Mystery:

Halloween Hijinks
The Trouble With Turkeys
Christmas Crazy
Cupid's Curse
Big Bunny Bump-off
Beach Blanket Barbie
Maui Madness
Derby Divas
Haunted Hamlet
Turkeys, Tuxes, and Tabbies
Christmas Cozy
Alaskan Alliance
Matrimony Meltdown
Soul Surrender
Heavenly Honeymoon
Hopscotch Homicide – *August 2015*
Ghostly Graveyard – *October 2015*
Santa Sleuth – *December 2015*

Paradise Lake Cozy Mystery:

Pumpkins in Paradise
Snowmen in Paradise
Bikinis in Paradise
Christmas in Paradise
Puppies in Paradise
Halloween in Paradise – *August 2015*

Whales and Tails Cozy Mystery:

Romeow and Juliet
The Mad Catter
Grimm's Furry Tail
Much Ado About Felines – *July 2015*
Legend of Tabby Hollow – *September 2015*
Cat of Christmas Past – *November 2015*

Seacliff High Mystery:

The Secret
The Curse
The Relic – *July 2015*
The Conspiracy – *October 2015*

Road to Christmas Romance:

Road to Christmas Past

Chapter 1

Tuesday, July 28

I glared at the rusty bucket that was relegated to the far corner of the dark, windowless room. An expressionless man had brought it to me after I'd informed my captor that there were certain urges that needed tending to. I'm not a prude and am normally more than willing to adapt to any situation, but even I have my limits. As I paced back and forth across the filthy stone floor of the small room, I focused all my energy on chanting the mantra that currently served as the only thing standing between my self-respect and my complete and total degradation.

"I do not have to pee, I do not have to pee, I do not have to pee."

Who was I kidding? I totally had to pee.

I don't know what I expected from my honeymoon. Moonlight walks on the beach, romantic dinners by candlelight, time with the people who meant the most to me. What I didn't expect was to spend my second night on Heavenly Island in a bug-infested jail cell dressed in nothing more than a thin red minidress. Maybe I should have been prepared for the fact that Zoe Donovan, who I guess should now be Zoe Donovan-Zimmerman, would end up knee deep in the middle of the first murder the island had seen in a decade.

Talk about the perfect end to the past forty-eight perfectly horrid hours. Okay, maybe they weren't *all* horrid. There were some really good moments mixed in with some not so good ones. But as far as honeymoons go, I'd had my share of problems. I guess if I was being perfectly honest I knew deep in my gut that something like this was coming.

"The interrogator will see you now," a short man with a rotund belly, small bulging eyes, and chubby cheeks announced.

Interrogator? That didn't sound good at all.

"Where exactly am I?" I asked the man as I followed him down the dark, narrow hallway to a dark, narrow room.

"You are in jail. I figured you knew."

"I know I'm in jail, but where exactly am I on the island? Am I still on the resort?"

"No, ma'am." The man indicated that I should take a seat at the rickety table that had been leveled with a matchbook. "You are in Hades."

"Hades?" Well, I guess that explained the décor. "And where exactly is Hades?"

The man's face clearly indicated his irritation at my questions, but he answered anyway. "The island is made up of two parts. The western half of the island is populated by rich and snooty people such as yourself who have come to the Heavenly Island Resort to be pampered and waited on by those of us who live on the eastern half of the island."

"I see. I guess it makes sense that the people who work at the resort must live somewhere outside the resort. But why Hades?"

The man just raised his eyebrow.

"Yeah, I guess it must suck to spend your whole day pampering us rich and snooty types and then return home every night to less-than-ideal living conditions. Do you work for Jensen Ewing?" I mentioned the name of the resort owner.

The man spat on the ground. "I would never work for that dictator. The settlement of Hades exists independently of the resort. I work for the people I serve."

"I see. Well, thank you." I paused. "I'm sorry; what did you say your name was?"

"I didn't say. People call me Toad."

Toad? I suppose he did sort of look like a toad, with his compact yet portly frame and bulging eyes.

"Thank you, Toad," I replied. "I don't suppose I can use the bathroom before we get started?"

The man just grunted as he walked out of the door, leaving me alone in the room, which smelled of smoke, urine, and despair. My greatest hope for the moment was that I wouldn't be left sitting in the room long enough to add to the stench.

I crossed my legs and prayed for a superhuman level of control over my bladder. I never should have had that last glass of wine. If only I'd known that, in spite of everything that had happened, it would be those seemingly harmless six ounces that would send me toward a complete and total breakdown.

I wished I could blame my current situation on a faulty Zodar system, but honestly, my instinct has been as accurate as ever. It was my interpretation of the wave of trepidation I felt as I watched the last of our wedding guests drive away that let me down. At the time I'd attributed my prophetic chills to the fact that Levi Denton and Ellie Davis, my very best friends in the world, had decided not to come on the trip as planned. I was disappointed by the news but not really surprised. I knew Levi wanted to make a trip to the university where he'd been offered a job on the coaching staff of the football team, and Ellie had decided to go with him.

I guess I can understand how the real-life decisions facing the couple would take precedence over a trip to a tropical island where, according to the brochure, all your fantasies are guaranteed to come true. The island was beautiful, but so far it had been nightmares rather than fantasies that were coming to pass.

I uncrossed and then recrossed my legs as I looked around the room. At this point a rusty bucket would look pretty darn good. Unfortunately, the room was devoid of even the crudest of conveniences. Luckily, I only had to wait for a few minutes for a tall man with a chiseled chin and dark slate eyes to join me. He wasn't quite as scary-looking as the man who had shown me to the room, but he was a lot more intimidating, with his dark stare and serious expression.

I know in this situation I should play it cool and answer only the questions directed at me. I could hear Zak's voice in my head cautioning me to wait for the man who had joined me to set the pace. Of course anyone who knows me knows I rarely play it cool and controlled.

"Please. I know how it looks, but you have to believe me. I didn't kill Ricardo Jimenez," I blurted out before the man even sat down. "Yes, I argued with him just an hour before he was murdered, and yes, I even threatened to do him bodily harm, but I didn't kill him, despite the fact that I had both motive and opportunity."

I swear the man's expression didn't change even a tiny bit throughout my outburst. He sat down on a hard metal chair across from me as if I had never spoken. He looked me up and down, but he didn't say anything.

"Look, I know how it looks. I really do," I rambled on. "I know I'm rambling and I know I keep repeating myself, but you have to believe I would never kill anyone. I'm a nice person. Really. Ask around. Please, you have to let me out of here."

The man tapped his left index finger on the table in a steady rhythm that seemed to indicate his boredom, but still he didn't respond. I was beginning to suspect his preferred interrogation method was *torture them with silence*. It was working.

"I know. I just need to calm down and let you ask the questions. Right?"

The man narrowed his gaze but still didn't speak.

"I don't suppose I can use a bathroom before we begin?" I asked hopefully.

"No, I don't suppose you can."

"But I'm really not sure I can hold it," I pleaded.

The man shrugged. "We can hose down the floor if we have to."

Great.

"You seem healthy and physically fit," the man stated.

"I don't see what that has to do with anything, but yes, I run almost every day."

"So you were physically capable of plunging a knife into the victim's back."

"Well, yes, I suppose. But he was tall and I'm short. I would have had to stand on a stool to get the leverage I would have needed to plunge the knife into him at the angle at which the knife was plunged, so really I couldn't have killed him."

The man glared at me, but he seemed to be considering my statement.

"If you didn't kill this man why don't you tell me what *did* happen," the man suggested.

I let out a long breath. At least he was going to give me the opportunity to tell my side of the story before he tossed me in a cell, locked the door, and threw away the key.

"I went up onto the deck after dinner," I began.

"Start at the beginning," the man interrupted.

"From my arrival on the boat?"

"From your arrival on the island."

Oh, *that* beginning. I could see this was going to be a long conversation.

"Are you sure we can't take a short break so I can use the bathroom?"

"I'm sure."

Wonderful.

"My husband, Zak Zimmerman, and I arrived on Heavenly Island yesterday morning with two children who are visiting us for the summer."

"You brought children on your honeymoon?" he interrupted.

"Yes. Scooter Sherwood and his friend, Alex Bremmerton. We don't get to see them all that often, and when Mr. Ewing offered to let us use the big guesthouse, we decided to have a family vacation of sorts, even though we aren't a traditional sort of family. We arrived at the resort and were shown to the house, we settled in, and then we headed to the beach, where I met Ricardo."

"Ricardo Jimenez, the victim?" the interrogator specified.

"Yes, the victim. We're never going to get through this if you keep interrupting."

The man just smiled.

"Anyway, Ricardo came over to the lounge chair I was sitting on and asked me if I wanted to go to the bar for a drink. I explained that I was married and that my husband was swimming with the children but would be back shortly. The man didn't want to take no for an answer and sat down on the lounger Zak had been using. It was then that my dog Charlie, who had been napping in the shade under my chair, began barking at him. The man kicked sand at Charlie and Charlie snapped at him."

"He bit him?"

"No," I clarified, "he didn't bite him; he just snapped at him. Charlie is very protective of me, and it was obvious he didn't like the man."

"And where is this Charlie now?"

"At the house. I left him with Scooter, Alex, and Oria, the babysitter the resort provided, while Zak and I went on the dinner cruise."

"What happened after Charlie snapped at Mr. Jimenez?" the interrogator asked.

"The man kicked Charlie in the ribs and then walked away."

The interrogator frowned. "Is this Charlie okay?"

"Yeah, he's okay. Charlie was pretty shaken up, but the island veterinarian assured me that he wasn't in any way injured. I guess Charlie moved at the last minute so the man just grazed him."

The interrogator leaned back in his chair and looked me up and down. I had to admit that if my urge to pee wasn't making me squirm his intcnse stare would have. In spite of my resolve to wait, I couldn't take it one more minute. I jumped up from my chair and frantically looked around the room. "Please, I *really* need to visit the ladies' room."

The man didn't respond.

"I'm sorry I snubbed my nose at the bucket." I tried for my best I'm-sorry face. "Please. I'll only be a minute."

The man shrugged. "Very well. But leave the door open."

Thank God.

I wanted to argue about the open door, but I figured an open door was better than no door at all. The man led me down the hall to a small room that smelled like . . . well, let's not describe what it smelled like. Let's just say the aroma created by the turkey farm I worked on a couple of years ago didn't compare to the stench of the filthy room.

I looked for a toilet seat cover. There was none. I looked for toilet paper. Likewise absent. There was an old newspaper sitting on the edge of the filthy sink. I held my breath and did the best I could with what I had at my disposal. I knew the interrogator was waiting just outside the open door, but at least he stood with his back to me.

"Thank you." I smiled at the man who had taken mercy on me after I exited the room.

He nodded and ushered me back to the interrogation room.

"So after the incident on the beach," the man jumped right back in once we were settled, "when was the next time you saw Mr. Jimenez?"

I cringed. I hated to answer the question. "Later that night. Zak, the kids, and I decided to go to dinner at the oceanfront steak house in the main part of the resort. We were seated at a table on the lanai overlooking the beach, where I saw the man who had kicked Charlie talking to a dark-skinned man dressed in black. They appeared to be having a fairly intense conversation."

"Could you hear what they were saying?"

"No, they were too far away. After they finished speaking, the man who assaulted my dog headed toward the walkway that runs from the restaurant to the condos that line the beach. I excused myself on the pretext of using the ladies' room and went to head him off. I told him that if he got within twenty feet of my dog again I would make him wish he had never been born. He laughed and threatened to make a kabob out of Charlie, so I kicked him."

"Kicked him where?"

"You know." I blushed. "In the private parts."

The interrogator laughed. "And then?"

"And then I returned to the table and had a wonderful seafood dinner."

The interrogator made a pyramid with his fingers and then tapped the ends together in rhythmic repetition. I could tell he was processing what I'd told him and was most likely trying to make up his mind as to whether or not I was a killer. I focused on a fly that was circling the man's head in an effort to wait for the next question, rather than just ramble on, as I'd promised myself not to do.

I wondered what had happened to Zak. The last time I'd seen him was when the yacht docked and I was escorted away. He'd assured me that he'd have me out of jail in no time, but it had been at least a couple of hours and here I still sat.

"This occurred on Monday?" the interrogator finally asked.

"Yes."

"And when did you see Mr. Jimenez again after the incident outside the restaurant?"

"The next day," I admitted. "The next morning, to be more accurate. I don't believe he saw me, but I can't be certain."

I coughed and tried to clear my throat. The room was veiled in a thick layer of dust that wasn't helping my sinuses, which were already irritated due to the dry air.

"Do you need some water?" the man asked.

"No, thank you. I'm fine."

I *was* thirsty, but I was pretty sure I'd rather die of dehydration than risk a revisit to the ladies' room.

"Okay, then. Tell me about seeing the victim the morning after your encounter outside the restaurant."

I took a deep breath and settled in for what I assumed was going to turn into an endless narration, based on the way the man kept interrupting the flow of the conversation. Why hadn't I listened to Zak and stayed away from Ricardo, as he'd warned me to do? Even the most moronic of investigators was going to realize I had been at war with the man since the moment I'd arrived on the island.

"Charlie and I were out jogging," I continued. "We'd been running on the sand, but it was already getting crowded on the beach, so we decided to circle back and take the path that parallels the golf course. It was early, but there were still a surprisingly large number of people out and about. I decided to cut through the wooded area that runs behind the clubhouse when I saw Mr. Jimenez arguing with a woman. I stopped running in order to figure out an alternate route. The last thing I wanted to do was have another confrontation with the guy. While I was looking around to see if I could spot a relatively brush-free route to take, the man grabbed the woman by the arm and pulled her into a breezeway. I was afraid he was going to hurt her, so I snuck quietly toward the building. I was afraid Charlie was going to bark and give away our location, so I was hesitant to get too close. I was trying to decide what to do when I saw Mr. Jimenez walking down the path toward the hotel. He was alone. I went over to the breezeway, but it was empty, so I continued on my way."

The man narrowed his gaze. "You didn't see the woman leave?"

"No. She must have used the breezeway to access one of the paths leading back toward the other end of the resort."

The interrogator pulled a toothpick out of his pocket. He rolled it between his fingers before using it to pick something from between his two front teeth. He then stuck the toothpick between two of his back teeth and closed his mouth around it.

"Can you describe this woman?" the man asked after almost a minute of silence.

"Tall. Thin. Long dark hair. I didn't catch her eye color, but her skin was a dark brown, so I imagine her eyes were dark as well. She wore a business suit. A knee-length skirt with a short jacket. I think it was dark gray. It could have been black. Her shoes were dark as well. To be honest, it occurred to me that she looked out of place. I mean, those heels? Really? She certainly wasn't going to walk through the sand in those things."

"It sounds like you're referring to Chandella. She's Mr. Ewing's mistress."

"Mr. Ewing has a mistress? He seems so nice."

"Nice people can't have mistresses?"

I thought about Zak's tall and handsome friend. He had a petite wife with a welcoming smile who appeared to be at least six months pregnant.

"No," I decided. "They can't."

"Mr. Ewing is a very wealthy man."

"So?" I really didn't see what being wealthy had to do with being a cheating lowlife.

"So he can afford to support many women. I believe Chandella is only one of his women."

I frowned. I didn't realize women were a commodity that could be collected based on one's ability to provide for them.

"Don't worry. He takes good care of the mother of his child. She won't be left wanting."

I wasn't sure that was the point but decided not to say as much.

"When did you next see Mr. Jimenez?" the investigator asked.

"Later that afternoon. Zak and I took the kids to the pool."

"You're staying in the VIP section of the resort?"

"VIP section?" I asked.

"The VIP section is reserved for celebrities and very rich guests. It's gated and can be accessed only with a VIP key."

"Oh, yeah, I guess we are staying in the VIP section. I was wondering about the extra gate."

"And the pool you were swimming in. Was it the VIP pool?"

"No. The kids prefer the bigger pool near the clubhouse. Is this relevant?"

The interrogator shrugged. "Go on."

"Anyway, Zak and the kids were swimming while I caught up on some reading. We'd left Charlie at the house because dogs aren't allowed in the pool area. I began to feel bad about leaving him alone in a strange environment, so I decided to head back early. I saw Mr. Jimenez speaking to a large man wearing a brightly colored Hawaiian-style shirt as I passed the clubhouse. The man with the Hawaiian shirt had a dog by his side. The dog looked as if it had been abused. I know I should have just minded my own business, but I can't stand to see an animal in pain, so I approached the pair and suggested to them that the man really should seek medical attention for the large gash on the dog's shoulder."

"I take it the man didn't welcome your advice."

"No, he just laughed at me and told me to mind my own business. I threatened to report him to the authorities and he laughed harder."

"While most of the citizens of the island are caring and responsible pet owners, I'm afraid we don't have the same abuse laws here that you have in your country." The man looked genuinely dismayed by that fact. I had to admit I was beginning to like the guy.

"So after the men laughed at you, then what happened?"

"I made a few comments about the humane treatment of animals and the man with the dog threatened to toss me in with a couple of the dogs I was arguing to protect, so I could see for myself that they weren't the cuddly puppies I imagined."

"Did the men physically injure or assault you?"

"No. They just made rude and threatening comments and blocked my attempt to continue on my way. Eventually, another man came along and told them to cool it."

The interrogator frowned. "And this other man— can you describe him?"

"He was tall and portly, with white hair. He had a tattoo of a sea serpent on his shoulder."

"It sounds like Captain Jack. Captain Jack pilots Mr. Ewing's yacht."

I knew Captain Jack had been on the yacht tonight. I hadn't met him, but the man I met on the beach looked the type to be a crusty old sea dog. It was reasonable to believe they were one and the same.

The interrogator took out a pad of paper and made some notes before he continued. I really wished he'd move things along. All I wanted to do at that point was to go back to the house and wrap myself in Zak's strong and protective arms.

"So the man in the brightly colored shirt—did you see him on the yacht tonight?"

"No. Although I didn't meet all the staff."

The interrogator jotted down a few more notes. "And after the incident on the beach, when was the next time you saw Mr. Jimenez?"

"Tonight on the yacht."

"And how did you come to be on the yacht?"

"Jensen Ewing invited Zak and me to a dinner party. I guess Zak and Jensen are business acquaintances of some sort, although I never did ask specifically how they knew each other."

The interrogator shoved a piece of paper in front of me. "These are the names of the people who were on the vessel when Mr. Jimenez was killed. Do they look right to you?"

I tried to remember who had been on the boat as I looked at the list. There'd been twelve diners that evening, sitting six to a side at a long table. Jensen Ewing and his wife Della sat in the middle of the table on the side nearest the kitchen. Ricardo Jimenez sat to Della's right, and next to him was his date, Stefana. They didn't seem to know each other all that well, so I'm going to guess she was a date of the escort variety. To Jensen's left was a British couple, Charles and Piper Belmont.

Zak and I sat on the other side of the table directly across from Jensen and Della. To Zak's left sat a delightful couple who were at the resort to celebrate their fiftieth wedding anniversary, Dezi and Lucinda Aquila. Seated to my right was a businessman from Korea named Park Lee, who was in attendance with his wife, Kim.

All twelve names were on the list, as were the names of the captain, chef, and staff. In all, there had been seventeen people on board when Ricardo Jimenez was stabbed.

"As I mentioned, I didn't meet all the staff, so I can't verify their names, but the names of the guests are correct, and the number of staff members listed looks right," I confirmed.

"Okay, then, walk me through the evening."

I sighed. "Have you spoken to my husband?"

"I have. He's been waiting in the lobby since you were brought in. Other than spending an inordinate amount of time on his phone, he has mostly just been pacing."

"Can I see him?"

"Perhaps when we're done. So, again, walk me through the evening."

I shifted in my chair. Would it kill them to provide padded chairs? I looked around the filthy room. On the other hand, maybe metal was better. Nowhere for creepy crawlies to hide. The staff at the resort had been friendly and clean-cut. I had to wonder if the entire village of Hades was as dingy as the jail.

Chapter 2

"Do you mind if I ask you a question before I continue?" I asked.

The interrogator shrugged. "Ask away."

"What's your name?"

The man looked surprised by my question. "Talin. Why do you ask?"

"It seems like we're in for a long discussion and I like to have a name to go with a face. Talin is a nice name. Very rugged. Is it okay if I refer to you as Talin?"

"Are you flirting with me so I'll go easy on you?"

"No," I assured the man. "Not flirting. I'm just trying to make the best of a really bad situation."

The man narrowed his gaze. I could see he was as ready for this interview to be over as I was. I tried to figure out how long I'd been in this hellhole. Several hours at least. Maybe more. When they'd first brought me in they'd tossed me in the dark cell without so much as a window. There really hadn't been any way to gauge the passage of time.

"As long as you get on with your story, you can call me anything you like," the man finally answered.

"Can I ask one more thing?"

The man sighed. "Very well, but just one more question and then you continue."

"The man who escorted me to the room—I believe his name is Toad—indicated that the local population lives in a village known as Hades. He indicated that most of the citizens of the settlement work at the resort. Everyone I've come into contact with at the resort has been extremely nice and helpful, yet I get the feeling there's disquiet between the locals and the resort's owner."

"When Mr. Ewing bought the land on which the resort is now located he forced everyone who was living there to move to the east side of the island. On one hand, he provided both jobs and housing for a very poor society. On the other, he completely disrupted the existing culture and social structure. He now sits on a throne of his own making and rules over those he can. Some of the locals love him; others hate him. Now, can we continue?"

"Absolutely. I'm sorry. Where were we?"

"You arrived at the boat. . . ."

"Yes, the boat."

I tried to visualize the huge yacht that was larger than most peoples' houses. It had three levels. The top deck was outfitted with tables, chairs, and loungers on which a passenger could soak up the sun. At the back of the top deck, behind the bridge, was a helicopter pad. The level below the deck held a common area that consisted of a large seating area, a dining room, an office, a bathroom, and a kitchen. Below that were bedrooms and bathrooms. I never did have the opportunity to venture to the lowest deck, but I got the impression that there was plenty of sleeping space for both a large crew and many guests.

I took a deep breath and dove in. "Zak and I arrived at the boat at seven thirty, as we were instructed to do by Mr. Ewing. When we boarded I believe everyone except Ricardo and Stefana were already on board because the boat pulled away from the dock just after they boarded. When I saw Ricardo I almost bolted, but Zak encouraged me to ignore the man. He assured me that we would have a wonderful time, that we shouldn't let him ruin our evening. I know Ricardo recognized me, but it appeared he'd likewise decided to play it cool. When we were introduced he acted as if we'd never met and I did the same."

"Did you speak to him after you were introduced?"

"Not at that point. The waiter brought us drinks and we mingled with the other guests, all of whom seemed very nice."

"Did you speak to anyone?" Talin asked.

"I hit if off right away with Dezi and Lucinda and spent most of my time talking to them, while Zak mingled a bit more extensively."

"Dezi and Lucinda were the couple celebrating their wedding anniversary?"

"Yes. When they found out that Zak and I were on our honeymoon they were more than willing to share small bits of advice on marriage and relationships in general. It was really a very enlightening conversation. I have to admit I learned a lot about what it means to really commit to a relationship from this very sweet couple."

"And the victim—did he appear to have engaged in any extensive conversations?"

I thought about the movement of the guests that evening. I'd been trying to ignore the dog abuser, so I hadn't paid any attention to him or who he spoke to, but I did remember he went up to the top deck with Della at one point. They weren't gone all that long and when they returned he grabbed Stefana and sat down at the bar. I explained all of this and more in great detail to the rugged man, who kept interrupting my narrative. I swear, at the rate we were progressing I was going to die of old age before this interview concluded.

"So after speaking to Della, Mr. Jimenez stayed at the bar with Stefana until dinner?" Talin asked.

"Yes. I never saw him leave the bar."

"And then?"

"Then we enjoyed a delicious meal."

I could feel my throat becoming raspy. There was no way around it; I was going to have to risk another trip to the ladies' room.

"You know, maybe I will take that water you offered earlier. I don't think I can go on if I don't wet my throat."

"Very well. I will fetch you some water, but you are to remain seated. I could handcuff you to the chair or I could trust you to do as I say."

"I'll stay seated. I promise."

That seemed to satisfy him because he left my hands free while he exited the room. I wished I could talk to Zak. In spite of the fact that Talin seemed to be nicer than I'd originally thought, I was really scared. If Zak had been on the phone the entire time I'd been locked up I was pretty sure the cavalry was on the way. I seemed to make a habit of getting into trouble, but Zak was equally skilled at rescuing me. I only needed to wait for my knight to break through the door and whisk me to safety.

While the outcome of this endless conversation was directly tied to my freedom, which terrified me, I'd learned a lot of interesting facts as well. Prior to my discussion with Toad, and now Talin, I'd never once stopped to consider the socioeconomic reality that had to exist to make a five-star resort such as Heavenly Island possible. Talin indicated that there was a level of unhappiness among the people who had lived on the island before the resort had been built, but I had to wonder if the unrest wasn't just a tad more intense than he'd indicated.

I didn't have long to ponder that question because, surprisingly, Talin returned quickly with not only water but bottled water. I wanted to hug the man for his generous gesture but decided not to make a fuss that could end up backfiring.

"Thank you." I opened the bottle and took a sip. It tasted like manna from heaven.

"Please continue with your story," Talin directed. "What happened after your lovely meal?"

"After dinner some of the men went up on the deck to smoke cigars, and many of the women followed them. Zak doesn't smoke, but he wanted to speak to Charles about a business opportunity, so I agreed to meet him on the deck after I used the ladies' room. While I was washing my hands I heard Ricardo speaking to another man in the hallway just outside the door. I honestly don't know who the second man was; I didn't recognize his voice. The men seemed to be planning to engage in some sort of betting operation that revolved around a dog fight. I'm afraid I went just a tiny bit ballistic. I had let that particular wound fester all afternoon and I was determined to speak my mind. By the time I dried my hands and left the ladies' room, Ricardo had made his way up to the deck. I don't know where the other man had gone off to, but I'm afraid I totally laid in to the dog-hating Mr. Jimenez."

"Laid in to him?"

"Verbally. I didn't kick him again, although I wanted to. I guess I said some things that might be considered to be threats."

Talin looked down at his notes. "Three of the other guests reported that you threatened to beat him with a chain."

"Yeah." I blushed. "I guess I did say that."

"Five of the guests reported that you called the man 'bottom-feeding pond scum' and you hoped 'he'd wake up the next day with an advanced case of leprosy.'"

"Yes, I said that as well. I said a lot of things I actually meant but shouldn't have said in public. I also said I hoped his man part would shrivel up and fall off. That actually got quite a few snickers from the people who witnessed my meltdown."

Talin smiled but didn't respond. He looked down at his notes. "I understand your anger. I too have no patience for animal abuse. However, there were eight guests on board this evening who reported you told Mr. Jimenez that he should sleep with one eye open as long as you were on the island. Given the fact that Mr. Jimenez didn't make it through the cruise alive, that's a threat I must take seriously."

I groaned. "I know I should never have said that. It really wasn't my finest moment. I said a lot of things I regret. But I was mad. *Really* mad."

"Did you take your anger one step further and stab the man?" Talin glared at me in a less than friendly manner.

"No. I swear. Zak suggested we go inside, so we did. The others wandered back inside shortly after that as well. After my outburst Zak pretty much glued himself to my side for the rest of the evening. We would have left, but we were in the middle of the ocean, so there was really nowhere to go."

"I have seven witnesses who stated that Mr. Jimenez left the room soon after everyone came back inside. You left the room alone sometime after that."

I closed my eyes and prayed for mercy from this rigid man. There was no way around it. Things were going to look bad.

"Mrs. Zimmerman . . ."

I opened my eyes and looked at him. "I'm sorry; I was praying. What I'm about to tell you is going to make me sound guilty, but please keep in mind that I really am innocent."

Talin didn't say anything, so I decided to take a leap of faith and plunge ahead.

"Dezi surprised Lucinda with a cake for their anniversary," I began. "One of the waitstaff left it on the table while we were all on the deck, but only a small portion of it had been sliced. The knife that had been left to cut the remainder of the cake, should we need it, had disappeared. Park decided he wanted a second piece, so I volunteered to go to the kitchen to find a knife to replace the one that had vanished."

"The knife that had vanished where?"

"I don't know. It was there one minute and gone the next. Maybe one of the staff came in while we were all talking. Anyway, the kitchen was deserted when I got there, so I picked up a knife that was sitting on the counter and started back toward the dining area. I passed one of the waiters in the hall who told me I had the wrong knife. He took the knife from me and then offered to bring the correct utensil out to the table. I returned to the lounge and waited, but he never brought the knife, so I decided to go back for it. When I was on my way back to the kitchen I found Ricardo in the hallway with a knife in his back. I'm pretty sure it was the same knife the waiter had taken from me. I pulled the knife out and turned Ricardo over with the intention of trying CPR. That was how Kim found me: kneeling on the floor in front of Ricardo's body with the bloody knife in my hand. But I didn't kill him. I swear."

"And the man you gave the knife to? What did he look like?"

"He was a tall, thin man with dark skin and dark hair. He might have been the man I saw Ricardo speaking to that first night I was on the island, but I don't know for certain. I honestly didn't pay all that much attention to details. I do remember that he had on black pants and a black shirt, which was what the man on the beach had been wearing. I imagine he must have been one of the kitchen staff who I hadn't met yet."

"I spoke to every single person on board as they left the boat," Talin informed me. "There were no passengers on board who fit your description. The only members of the staff or guests with dark skin were Rosa and Jerrell, and they both wore white."

"No, it wasn't either Rosa or Jerrell. It wasn't anyone I'd met that night."

Talin shoved the list in front of me again. "Who hadn't you met?"

I studied the names. "I met all the guests of course. Jerrell tended bar and Kai and Rosa served the meal. I didn't meet the chef, Sebastian, or the captain. If Captain Jack is the man I saw on the beach, as you indicated, the man I saw must have been Chef Sebastian."

"Sebastian is Polish. He has fair skin and light hair."

"So it wasn't him. It had to be someone who isn't on your list."

"There was no one aboard who isn't on this list. I had the entire vessel searched when it docked. I interviewed each person as they disembarked. I asked every person to list the people with whom they came into contact that evening. I can assure you there was no one aboard fitting your description."

"There had to be. I saw him."

"I'm afraid you are mistaken."

I frowned. "Something isn't right. I know what I saw."

"Were you drinking during the cruise?"

"Yes. Everyone had drinks before dinner and wine with dinner, but I wasn't drunk. I remember what I saw."

"According to everyone other than you, the man you say you gave the knife to doesn't fit the description of anyone on the yacht. The only conclusion I can come to is that you are the one who used the knife."

I put my hands over my face. This was looking bad. Really bad. My only alibi for the time of the murdered man's death was someone who apparently was a figment of my imagination.

"Look," I pleaded, "I know how it looks. I really do. But I didn't kill Ricardo Jimenez. Yes, I was angry with him, and yes, I threatened to carry out all sorts of heinous crimes against him, but I promise that my threats were simply that: threats."

"At this point you're our only suspect. I don't see that I have much choice other than to detain you until we can figure things out."

"There were seventeen people on board the yacht tonight. Why am I the only suspect?"

"It seems you were the only one who was absent from the lounge other than Mr. Jimenez."

"That's not true. Jimenez left the lounge before I went for the knife. I don't know where he went and I didn't see him between the lounge and the kitchen, but he wasn't in either place. When I got back to the lounge after trying to retrieve the knife the first time, Park wasn't there. I'm pretty sure both Charles and Jensen Ewing disappeared for a short time during that period as well. And neither the chef nor the two servers were in either the kitchen or the lounge. By my calculation that makes seven of us who had the opportunity to kill Jimenez. If you include the man I saw in the hall that makes eight."

"The man you met in the hall who took the knife from you but apparently doesn't exist?"

"He exists. I know what I saw."

"Perhaps. But still, at this point you seem the most likely suspect."

I closed my eyes against the tears that were threatening to fall. I really didn't know what more I could say. I was about to try one last time to reason with the man when Toad came in and whispered something in Talin's ear. Toad handed Talin the phone. He left the room, so I couldn't hear his end of the conversation, but he'd left the door open so I could watch his face as he spoke.

He was smiling. Eventually, the smile gave way to laughter. His face had softened quite a lot. I only hoped his change in mood was in some way connected to me. He hung up the phone and returned to the room where I was waiting.

"I just had a very enlightening conversation with a Sheriff Salinger from your hometown of Ashton Falls."

"How did he know I was here?"

"I imagine your husband called him. He has assured me that this isn't the first time you've been the prime suspect in a murder investigation. It seems you're a bit of a hothead."

"Maybe. But I'm an innocent hothead."

"This Sheriff Salinger must really like you. He has personally guaranteed your innocence. Combined with the fistful of hundred-dollar bills your husband offered as bail money, I'm inclined to let you go under three conditions."

"What conditions?" To be honest, I didn't really care. I just wanted out of there.

"You will promise not to leave the island until I indicate that it's all right for you to do so."

"Agreed."

"You will promise to check in with one of our detectives twice every day."

That sounded easy enough. "Who should I check in with?"

The man thought about it for a minute. "I believe Toad will be able to adequately serve this need as he's here most days."

"Okay, I'll check in with Toad twice every day. What's the third condition?"

"You must stay away from this investigation."

Uh-oh.

"Your Sheriff Salinger tells me that you like to meddle."

"It's not so much that I meddle; it's more that I seem to stumble across clues. Really, it's more a case of them finding me than me finding them."

"If you should stumble across a clue you are to come to tell Toad immediately. If I find that you've been snooping around without keeping Toad in the loop I'll put you in jail immediately. Do you understand?"

"Yes," I regrettably answered. "I understand."

Chapter 3

Wednesday, July 29

After signing a ridiculous amount of paperwork, I was allowed to return to the guesthouse, where I tossed and turned all night. I finally decided that the only solution to my current dilemma was to figure out who'd actually killed Ricardo Jimenez. I know Talin had warned me to stay out of the investigation, but I had very little confidence in Toad's ability to solve the case on his own. Talin did say that he'd toss me in jail if he found out I was snooping around without keeping Toad in the loop. To my way of thinking, that simply meant that for the duration of the investigation Toad was going to be my hopefully silent partner.

Of course I did need to figure out a way to fit investigating into sharing a fun, family-style vacation with the people who meant the most to me. Zak and the kids would be disappointed if I spent all of my time with my new buddy Toad.

"Good morning, Alex," I greeted the young girl who had acted as flower girl for our wedding along with Zak's dog, Bella. "I see you're writing in your journal."

Alex had confided that she'd started a diary after she'd read one written by a young girl who lived decades ago that she'd found in the attic of Zak's house during Christmas vacation. I'd learned that she was quite serious about anything she committed to doing, and she'd been entering her thoughts in the journal on a daily basis.

"Yes. I thought I'd take advantage of the quiet. The boys are in the pool."

By *boys*, she meant Zak and Scooter. Charlie had slept in with me and was currently standing by the door, waiting to be taken out.

"Did you have a nice time last night?" Alex asked as she completed her thought and then closed the journal.

"We did. The food was delicious and there was a very interesting couple there who were celebrating their fiftieth wedding anniversary."

Zak and I had decided not to mention the murder or my arrest until we could figure out how to tell the kids what had occurred without sending them into a panic. We didn't want them to hear about it from anyone else, however, so we were planning to sit them down and explain things later that afternoon, after Zak had a chance to do some digging.

"Wow. Fifty years. I hope I find someone who I can be happy with for fifty years. Do you think you'll still be married to Zak in fifty years?"

"Absolutely."

"I sometimes wonder if my parents will make it that long." Alex sighed.

"They seem to have a lot in common."

Alex's parents were archaeologists who traveled the world digging up rare artifacts. They were gone from Alex's life a lot more often than they were in it, which was one of the reasons I was committed to taking care of her myself. Still, they did seem to share a love for the lifestyle they'd chosen.

"They have their work, but sometimes it seems like their work is all they have. I found out recently that they only got married after they found out I was on the way. I guess I was an accident—an unwelcome accident who really didn't have a place in their lives from the very beginning."

"Oh, honey, I'm sure that isn't true."

Alex looked at me. "Actually, I think it is. I don't think they wanted me to know, but the last time I saw them they seemed even more preoccupied than usual. I asked my mom if everything was okay and she said it was, but I could tell it wasn't. I guess I pushed when I should have let it go, and she admitted she never really wanted to marry my dad. She said they made better friends than lovers. I asked her why they got married in the first place if that was true, and that's when she told me they got married because of me."

I sat down next to Alex. Charlie tilted his head, as if to inquire about the delay in my taking him out, but I knew that comforting Alex was more important. It seemed like her mom had dumped some pretty serious information on a mature girl who was still only a child.

"Even if your mom and dad did marry because of you I'm sure they both love you," I tried, even though, based on their actions, I wasn't certain that was true. "Adults sometimes have complicated emotional baggage that children aren't equipped to understand. I know you wish you could spend more time with your parents, but Zak and I are so very happy to have the opportunity to fill in when they aren't around."

Alex smiled. "I really love spending time with you and Zak too."

"How about we put serious thoughts on the back burner and focus on having a wonderful time during our family getaway?"

Alex hugged me, and my heart melted just a tiny bit more than it already had where she was concerned. There was no doubt about it: the girl had carved a permanent place in my heart.

"Did you have a nice time with Oria last night?" I asked, deciding to change the subject to something less stressful and confusing.

"We did." Alex brightened considerably. "She's really nice, and she invited us to go horseback riding with a group from Kids Club today."

Kids Club was an activity group that entertained kids from ages five to twelve during the day so their parents could partake of adult-type activities. So far we hadn't sent Scooter and Alex to the club, but this sounded like a wonderful way for them to be entertained while Zak and I investigated.

"Would you like to go horseback riding?" I asked after I clipped Charlie's leash onto his collar.

Alex hesitated. "Scooter and I want to do whatever you and Zak would like to do. It's your honeymoon, after all. But if you don't have plans, I do like to ride."

"I don't think we have plans today. How about I speak to Zak about it after I take Charlie out? What time is the group leaving?"

"The ride is from ten to four. They're bringing lunch for us."

"Sounds fun. It's only eight, so let me speak to Zak and then I'll let you know."

After taking Charlie for a short walk I tracked Zak and Scooter down at the pool. Scooter likewise was excited about the ride, and Zak thought it was a good way to give us some time alone, so I called Oria and made the arrangements for them to go. She asked us to meet her at the clubhouse a half hour early so she could get Scooter and Alex registered because they hadn't taken part in any club activities yet. I showered, dressed, and grabbed a quick bowl of cereal for breakfast, then accompanied Scooter and Alex to the clubhouse while Zak caught up on some phone calls.

"I'm so glad it worked out for you to come along," Oria greeted the kids.

Following my conversation with the law enforcement personnel in Hades regarding the discontent of many of the locals, I looked closer at Oria's smile in an attempt to discern whether it was authentic. On the surface at least, it seemed to be.

The tall blonde handed me a packet of paperwork. "These are just release forms and emergency contact information. If you could fill them out we'll be all set for any activities Scooter and Alex want to participate in with the club during your stay at the resort."

I took a pen from the cup on the table and began to write. "Have you worked here long?" I asked.

"Seven years."

"And you like what you do?"

"I love it," Oria gushed. "If I had to invent the perfect job this would be it. I get to live in a beautiful place where I have good friends who mean the world to me and, best of all, I get to work with kids all day. I really am in heaven."

The speech didn't *seem* rehearsed. The woman seemed genuinely happy.

"Do you live in Hades?" I asked as I continued to write.

"Yes. I have an apartment just a block from the beach. It's a two-bedroom, so I share it with my friend Leta."

"Does Leta also work at the resort?"

I turned to the second page of the registration packet. There was a lot of information requested that I could only guess at, but I did the best I could.

Oria nodded. "She works in guest services. You might have met her when you checked in. She's short and a little plump, but she has a great smile. She usually works the registration desk."

"I do remember her." I stopped writing and looked up. "She has short hair with highlights?"

"Yeah, that's her."

"She seemed friendly and welcoming. Does she love her job too?" I inquired.

Oria shrugged. "Maybe not as much as I do, but she likes her job okay. Leta grew up on the island, so she has a certain nostalgia for the way things were before the resort was built, while I only moved here to take the job with the resort, so I don't miss the old way of life. Still, I think she's mainly content."

"How long ago was the resort built?" I asked as I continued with the paperwork.

"It opened eighteen years ago, but they started construction several years before that."

"Someone told me the construction displaced some of the local families, who were forced to move from their homes to the other side of the island."

"Yes. Leta was only fourteen when the land the resort sits on was purchased. Her family had to move over to the east side of the island before construction got underway. Her parents were unhappy about it, but Leta said it wasn't so bad. The house they lived in before the resort came was old and in disrepair; the house they were relocated to was brand-new and much nicer."

"And her parents were unhappy?" I stopped writing and looked directly at Oria.

"The house they owned on the west side of the island was on a large piece of land. The new house was part of a housing tract. While the house itself was an upgrade, they lost the ability to raise animals and grow their own food. Which, in Leta's opinion, was fine because animals and a garden simply represented chores to a fourteen-year-old girl. Still, I guess her parents took the move pretty hard."

"And Leta's parents? Do they still live on the island?"

"They do. They still live in the same house they were given when they were forced to move."

"And do they work at the resort as well?"

"Her dad works in maintenance and her mom works in the laundry. Don't forget to add the medical information on the back of the second page. It's important that we know about allergies and medical limitations."

I looked down at the sheet where Oria was pointing. I really didn't know the answers to many of the questions. I looked at Alex. "Do you have any allergies?"

"No. Not that I know of."

I looked at Scooter "How about you?"

"The headmaster at school says I'm allergic to mornings and homework."

I smiled. "I don't think that's what they mean by allergies. Have either of you been in the hospital?"

Somehow, with the kids' help, I managed to get the form filled out. I explained to Oria that I wasn't the parent of the children, and although I'd been given permission by the parents to make emergency medical decisions, I didn't have firsthand knowledge of their medical situations. She said she'd keep that in mind.

"We'll be back at four," she informed me. "You can pick the children up here."

"Okay, great." I hugged both kids. "Have a wonderful time."

After I left the clubhouse I checked in with Toad, who reported that he had no news, and then headed back to the house with the intention of figuring out who killed Ricardo Jimenez. The key to solving the case seemed to lay with discovering the identity of the missing crew member. While identifying the man might seem like a long shot, Zak and I had solved other cases that seemed unsolvable, so I felt good about our chances. If we couldn't find the real killer I didn't know what I'd do. I certainly wasn't willing to go back to the dungeon the islanders referred to as a jail.

As I walked along the path that led to the house, I tried to clear my mind and focus on the beauty surrounding me. There were a few white, fluffy clouds on the horizon, but the sky was mostly a deep blue that matched the color of the endless sea almost perfectly. One of the guests last night—I believe it was Park Lee—mentioned something about a storm on the horizon, but I hadn't paid much attention, and it certainly hadn't shown up today.

The waves on this side of the island tended to lap effortlessly onto the white sand beach, while the ones on the back side were larger and favored by surfers. Zak liked to surf, but so far he hadn't had the chance to do so. I wondered if we'd have the opportunity to do any of the activities we'd planned to schedule into our week now that finding a killer had jetted to the top of the list.

I paused briefly at the top of the bluff, where the path changed direction and headed inland for a bit. I closed my eyes as I listened to the sound of the waves, which served as a backdrop for the seagulls who squawked as they competed for the small crabs that dotted the beach. I'd always loved the ocean— the smell of the salt as it mingled with the seagrass that washed onto the shore during the night, the heaviness of the air, moist with the humidity that can be found in a tropical environment, and the sound of children laughing as they played on the beach below the bluff on which I was standing.

I turned toward the interior of the island, which was thick with foliage, as I continued on my way. I hadn't seen any monkeys, but I'd been told that Jensen had imported some in order to give the island a wild and rugged feel. At first I hadn't been sure how I felt about importing animals that weren't indigenous to the area, but I'd since learned that the island had at one point been home to monkeys that were wiped out in an epidemic over seventy years earlier. Besides, the island was beautiful. I guess if I were a monkey I wouldn't mind living here.

As I continued on, I enjoyed the plethora of tropical birds that frequented the center of the island, where the beach gave way to an elevation in altitude, as well as dense foliage that seemed as deadly as it was beautiful. The path I traveled wound its way along the edge of the jungle before curving back toward the sea. I hoped I'd be given the opportunity to wander deeper into the island before we were scheduled to leave. If the birds and foliage along the perimeter of the jungle was this beautiful it must be breathtaking in the interior.

By the time I made it back to the house Zak was off the phone and walking on the beach in front of the house with Charlie. He was throwing a stick to my tiny friend, who was having a blast chasing it into the gentle surf.

"There's my beautiful bride." Zak pulled me into his arms and kissed me as I walked up behind him.

"Did you miss me?"

"You have no idea. You know, this is the first time we've truly been alone since we've been married."

"We've been alone." I kissed his neck to remind him of our wedding night.

"Alone behind a locked door with four other people in the house, but not alone alone."

"Yeah, I know what you mean. It is nice that the kids are occupied for the day. I wish we could just enjoy our alone time, but I really don't want to go back to that jail, so I think we might need to do some investigating."

"We will," Zak promised. "After."

"After what?"

"You'll see." He grinned as he pulled a backpack onto his shoulders and grabbed my hand. He led me to the gate dividing the VIP section from the rest of the resort and then past the gatehouse dividing the village from the resort toward a narrow path leading away from the sea, toward the interior of the island. Charlie followed along beside us, happily chasing birds as the open air of the sea gave way to the density of the large tropical plants that grew in abundance.

"Have you stopped to wonder about all the security the resort provides?" I asked as we wound our way through the thick foliage.

"What do you mean?" Zak asked.

"Not only is there an armed guard at the gatehouse that must be passed to gain entry to the resort but there's an additional gate separating the area where we're staying from the rest of the resort."

"The resort is frequented by wealthy people who come to the island to escape the rigors of everyday life. Visitors include public figures such as politicians and celebrities. I think Jensen just wants to make sure his guests are granted the privacy they seek."

"Yeah, I guess I can see that." I'd had very limited yet disastrous dealings with paparazzi; I couldn't imagine what it must be like to try to have a normal vacation if you were a famous movie star or athlete.

Zak continued to pull me deeper and deeper into the jungle. I could tell by the grin on his face that he was up to something special. "Where are we going?" I asked as I swatted at a spider of unknown origin that had found its way onto my arm.

"It's a surprise." Zak continued to pull me along by the hand.

"Is it far?"

"No. Actually, we're almost there. In fact, I think you can hear it now."

I paused to listen. "It sounds like water."

Zak began walking again and I followed along behind. The jungle was beautiful, but the farther we traveled away from the coolness of the sea breeze the hotter and more humid it became.

Eventually, we came to a gated area with "Private Property" signs lining the fence. Zak punched a code into the gate, which slid open. I followed him into the fenced-in area and the gate slid closed behind us.

"Is it okay that we're in here?" I asked.

"I cleared it with Jensen. In fact, it was his idea. There are parts of the island that are restricted from the resort guests, due mainly to the fragile ecosystem he's trying to preserve."

We walked for another ten minutes and then the jungle gave way to one of the most beautiful sights I had ever seen. A large waterfall cascaded down a small mountain and emptied into a pond. Flowering plants lined the pool, and perched in nearby trees were the monkeys I'd been hoping to see.

"Wow, this is beautiful."

Zak took my hand and pulled me toward the pool of clear, cool water.

"Are you sure we're alone?" I asked as he slid his hand up my back and under my shirt.

"I'm sure," Zak responded as he pulled my tank top over my head.

"And there are no cameras?" I couldn't help but remember the photo of me that had ended up in a popular gossip magazine the week before our wedding.

"No cameras and no spectators . . . well, except for the monkeys," Zak assured me as he continued to undress us both.

Once we were both free of our clothing we slipped into the cool water, which felt like heaven against my hot skin.

I put my arms around Zak's neck and kissed him. "You know, I think this is one of the best ideas you've ever had."

Zak grinned as he pulled me against his body. "Actually," he kissed his way down my neck and onto my shoulder, "I'm about to show you the best idea I've ever had."

"I can't remember the last time I was this relaxed," I said an hour later as Zak and I sat on beach towels he'd placed on a large flat rock. He really did have all sorts of good ideas.

"How are the sandwiches?" he asked as I devoured the lunch he'd prepared.

"Really good. Where did you get the fresh rolls?"

"I had some brought over from the restaurant. They threw in some pastries, which are some of the best I've ever tasted. I wasn't sure they'd survive the trip, so they're waiting for us at the house."

I must have let my smile slip as I remembered the murder investigation that was also waiting for us at the house because Zak squeezed my hand and reassured me that, one way or another, we were both getting off the island.

"It looks like there's a cave up there on the mountain," I commented as I tried to focus on enjoying the rest of our trip into the jungle.

Zak looked where I was pointing. "That must be the cave Jensen told me about. It's been outfitted to provide shelter for resort guests during hurricanes or tropical storms. I guess this mountain is the tallest on the island. We actually climbed almost a thousand feet up the mountain during our hike from the house, and the cave is another thousand feet up."

"Is the mountain accessible from other parts of the island?" I wondered.

Zak frowned. "I'm not sure. Why do you ask?"

"It's just that we had to go through the private gate to get here. I was just wondering where the locals went in a storm."

"Good question."

"Did you know that many of the locals refer to Jensen Ewing as the dictator?"

Zak hadn't heard, so I shared what I'd learned about the history of the resort and its impact on the island and the people who lived here before Jensen bought the land. I could see Zak hadn't really considered this side of things. His smile had faded to a frown by the time I'd completed my monologue.

"Not that there aren't locals who are happy that Jensen developed the island. Oria told me that her friend, Leta, was thrilled to move into the housing he provided when he built the resort, and I'm sure there are others as well. It's been eighteen years since the resort opened, and construction began several years before that, so I imagine folks have mostly settled into their new situation. Still, if it was Jensen who was dead and not Ricardo Jimenez, I would definitely look at the social climate as one of the top two motives."

"Top two? What other motive are you referring to?"

"Good old-fashioned jealousy. Did you know that Jensen has a mistress? More than one, it seems. Della is the mother of his child, but if what Talin told me is correct, she isn't his only lover."

Zak frowned. "I don't know Jensen all that well. We worked together on the software for the resort several years ago, but we never discussed anything really personal. Still, I have to admit I'm surprised. He seems to have genuine affection for Della."

"Talin indicated that having mistresses is almost expected when you have as much money as Jensen does."

Zak took my hand in his and looked me in the eye. "I have a lot more money than Jensen and I promise you that I have no plans to make room in our lives for a mistress."

I smiled. "Good."

"I guess we should head back," Zak suggested reluctantly. "We really do need to figure out who killed Jimenez before someone gets it in their head that you're a risk to the populace. I'm kind of surprised no one has been talking about the murder today. From what I can find out this is the first homicide in a decade. You'd think it would be big news."

"Jensen might have persuaded everyone to keep it hushed up. I can't imagine it would be a good thing for the resort guests to know they were trapped on the island with a killer. We really should talk to the kids when they get home from their ride."

Zak got up and began gathering our supplies. "Yeah, I agree. I think they'll take it okay as long as we keep a casual attitude about the whole thing. It seems like it should be fairly easy to figure this out. We were on a boat in the middle of the ocean with seventeen people on board. It's safe to assume Ricardo didn't stab himself in the back, and I'm also assuming neither you nor I did it, which leaves us with fourteen suspects. I bet we can narrow that down quite a bit if we put our minds to it."

"What about the man I saw? The one no one else did? He took the knife and said he would exchange it. It has to have been him who killed Ricardo."

Zak looked at me with a furrowed brow. "I'm not doubting that you saw a dark-skinned man dressed in black, but there doesn't currently seem to be any evidence to support it."

"I know what I saw."

"I believe you. I really do. It's just that after you were taken away they interviewed everyone, one person at a time. They left me until last, so I was able to watch each person as he or she was escorted into the office where the interviews took place. There really wasn't anyone who fit your description."

"Maybe he was hiding in one of the bedrooms."

"They searched the entire yacht. Thoroughly. The only people on board were the seventeen they've accounted for. If you did see a dark-skinned man dressed in black he somehow disappeared before the yacht docked."

"Maybe he dove overboard and swam to shore," I suggested.

Zak looked doubtful. Then he smiled and squeezed my hand. "Don't worry; we'll get to the bottom of this."

Chapter 4

After we returned to the house, showered, changed into clean clothes, and made a pitcher of sangria—who says you can't work and vacation at the same time?—Zak brought his computer out on to our private patio and set up a work station in the shade. We still had three hours until we needed to pick up the kids and we were determined to narrow the suspect field during that time.

Zak had managed to get the official list of passengers on board the yacht from Talin, so we decided that was as good a place as any to start. We'd been miles out to sea, so it only made sense that someone on the yacht had committed the deed.

"In addition to the twelve us of who dined that evening," Zak began, "there were five people on board."

I opened my mouth to speak.

"Six, if we include your mystery man."

I knew all that. I'd gone over it time and time again with Talin, but Zak hadn't been in the room at the time, so I sat quietly while he caught up. The first thing he did was pull up a blank document on his computer and begin listing the names, which included Zak and me; Jensen and Della; Ricardo and his date, Stefana; Dezi and Lucinda; Charles and Piper Belmont; and the businessman from Korea, Park Lee, and his wife, Kim.

Also on board were Captain Jack, Sebastian the chef, and his two waitstaff, Kai and Rosa. The bartender, Jerrell, and my mystery man rounded out the list. If you eliminated the victim, Zak, and myself, that gave us fourteen suspects. If you added in my mystery man that brought the total to fifteen.

"So where do we start?" I asked, once he'd keyboarded the list to his Word document.

"I think we have to begin with the victim. If we can learn why he was there and who he might have come into contact with before dinner, maybe we can uncover a motive."

Made sense to me.

"We know the guy was a lowlife jerk," I began.

Zak looked at me. "Should I add you back to the list?" he teased.

"No. I just don't like that he kicked Charlie, and I don't like that he bet on dog fights. The guy had no morals. Chandella," I shouted.

Zak looked confused. "I'm not following your line of reasoning. What is a chandella?"

"It's not a what, it's a who. She's Jensen's mistress, or at least one of them. I saw Ricardo arguing with a tall dark-haired woman when Charlie and I were out jogging yesterday. When I described her to Talin, he said it sounded like Chandella. I saw Ricardo grab her and drag her into a breezeway, but when I went to investigate she was gone. I saw him walking toward the hotel but didn't see where she disappeared to. She seemed pretty mad."

"Chandella wasn't on the yacht," Zak pointed out.

"No, but maybe Jensen found out that Ricardo was messing with his mistress and put an end to it."

Zak frowned. "I don't know. Jensen orchestrated the entire evening. He was responsible for everyone who was on board. Why would he participate in an act to defend his mistress with his wife on board?"

"Her presence suggests that jealousy wasn't a motive in Ricardo's death. Maybe she was a smoke screen. Maybe we all were."

"Maybe," Zak admitted. "We'll keep Jensen on the list, but I doubt Della did it. She's pretty far along in her pregnancy."

I thought about it. "Maybe she didn't plunge the knife into the man's back, but she could have been working with the killer. She certainly would have the ability to sneak someone on board ahead of time and then hide them so no one knew they were there. Someone like my dark-skinned man, for example."

"Okay, we'll leave her on the list for now," Zak agreed. "So back to Jimenez. Let's see if he'd been on the island before."

"How are you going to figure that out?" I asked.

"I can access passport information as well as resort records to see if he's stayed here before. It'll take a few minutes."

"He seemed to know a lot of people, so I'm betting he's a regular visitor. I think I'll call Ellie while you're doing that. I can't help but wonder how her trip is going. The suspense of not knowing is making me nuts."

"Okay. Tell her hi for me."

I took the phone and walked over to the rock wall separating the patio from the beach. I didn't want to disturb Zak while he worked and I didn't want to have to monitor what I said to my best friend. Zak tended to side with Levi in the fact that he believed the opportunity he was being offered was too good to pass up. I, on the other hand, sided with Ellie in her desire for the best friend unit to remain intact.

Besides, I really didn't see how Ellie could choose between her home and her boyfriend.

"So how are things going?" I asked as soon as she picked up.

"They're going. Levi met with the head coach yesterday and he really liked what he had to say. He promised me that he would sleep on it for a day or two, but I can tell he's already made up his mind. I overheard him talking to the new principal at the high school. He wouldn't share this information with him if he weren't planning to give notice."

I felt my heart sink. "What are you going to do?"

"I'm not sure what I'm going to do in the long run, but for now I'm staying put in Ashton Falls. I love Levi, but I love living in the boathouse and I love my business. My mom is in Ashton Falls, as is my best friend in the whole world. I don't see how I can leave."

I could tell that Ellie was crying, but I didn't say anything. I wished I could be there with her while she dealt with this life-altering situation.

"Have you told Levi that you aren't going to move with him?" I asked.

"Sort of. I told him that I wanted to stay in Ashton Falls. He thinks we can keep our relationship going long distance, and while I agree we can keep the friends part of us alive from four hundred miles apart, I really don't think we can keep the couple thing going."

I hated to admit it, but I had to agree with Ellie. Long-distance relationships rarely stood the test of time.

"Maybe he'll hate it," I suggested. "Maybe once he gets there the novelty will wear off and he'll want to come home."

"Maybe."

"Are you back in Ashton Falls?" I asked.

"I am. I flew home earlier today and Mom picked me up in Bryton Lake. Levi decided to stay for a few more days. He wanted a chance to actually work out with the team to get a feel for how everyone interacted before he officially quit his job at the high school. At first I was really upset that we weren't going to have this time together, but now I think it might be for the best. I need some time to process everything."

"I wish I could be there with you. I hate to think of you all alone. I'd come home early, but I've been forbidden to leave the island."

"Zoe Donovan, what did you do?"

"It's not what I actually did; it's more what everyone seems to think I did."

"Please don't tell me you're mixed up in a murder."

I remained silent. She'd said not to tell her.

"You *are* mixed up in a murder," Ellie concluded. "How on earth did you manage to do that? You've only been on the island for a couple of days."

I explained about the events leading up to my arrest and then I explained, in excruciatingly painful detail, about my horrible evening in jail.

"You used a newspaper as toilet paper?" Ellie laughed.

"It's not like I had a choice. I had on a tiny silk dress that barely covered anything, so I had on minimal undergarments, and I couldn't risk drippage."

Ellie laughed even harder. I was glad my horrible night could bring some light into her dark day. I guess, looking back, it *was* sort of funny, although it most definitely hadn't been amusing at the time.

"I should have come with you as planned." Ellie sighed. "It sounds like your murder investigation is a lot more interesting than my imploding romance."

"Maybe you can still come," I suggested. "If Coop isn't busy I'm sure Zak will send him to pick you up. You can be here by tomorrow morning. The fourth bedroom is totally empty."

"Do you have any idea how much that would cost?"

"Zak won't mind. Will you come?"

Ellie hesitated. I knew she was considering it. "I've already arranged for coverage at the restaurant, and I'm sure Tiffany won't mind if I take Shep back over to your place."

My assistant, Tiffany Middleton, was staying at the house to take care of Zak's dog Bella, as well as my cats, Marlow and Spade. She'd kept Levi's dog, Karloff, and Shep as well while they were visiting the college.

"El?" I persuaded.

"Okay. If Zak really doesn't mind paying a fortune for me to get there, and if Coop really is available."

"I'll check into it and call you back."

As expected, Zak was more than happy to send Coop for Ellie, and Coop was fine with fetching her. Although Coop owns a private jet service catering to businessmen on the go and has many clients, I'm pretty sure Zak is his best customer, so I was certain Coop would be willing to do anything within his power to keep him happy. I called Ellie back and informed her that Coop would be waiting for her at the Bryton Falls airport later that evening. It would be good to have her around while we tried to balance fun with investigation.

Then I called Jeremy Fisher, who had been doing such a fantastic job managing Zoe's Zoo that he no longer really needed me, though, if I was honest with myself, I still needed to be needed. Does that make any sense?

"Hey, Jeremy," I said when he answered the phone.

"Zoe, how's the trip?"

"Eventful." I filled him in.

"You need to be careful. Other countries don't have the same type of justice system we do. Proving guilt isn't necessarily a requirement for locking someone up."

"Trust me, I've thought of that. How are things at the Zoo?"

Jeremy filled me in on the two bear cubs that had been transferred out and the mountain lion that had been transferred in. "I got a call this morning, asking if we could take some rescues from a puppy mill that was recently shut down. We have room for fifteen dogs, but that will max us out. The woman I spoke to is looking to place forty dogs, so she's pretty desperate."

"Take them, have them checked out for health issues, and then put the word out that we have dogs to place. We already have a clinic planned for when I get back. If you need the extra space see if you can find a few locals to foster some of our longer-term residents."

"Okay, I'll call the woman back when we're done. She'll be relieved we can take so many."

"Sometimes I think we need to expand our domestic section to accommodate more animals, and then as soon as I actually start planning an expansion we empty out and have plenty of room."

"We normally have plenty of room," Jeremy reminded me. "It's all but impossible to plan for these brief influxes when there's a large rescue operation underway."

"Call Nick Benson," I suggested. 'The last time I spoke to him, he told me he was thinking about getting another dog. Maybe he's ready. And even if he isn't, maybe he'll be willing to foster a couple of dogs for the short term. I bet my pappy will foster a dog or two as well."

"I'll take care of everything," Jeremy assured me. "You enjoy your honeymoon. And Zoe . . . try to stay out of trouble."

"I will," I promised. "I'll call you in a couple of days."

I hung up with Jeremy and returned to Zak, who'd managed to dig up some information on our murder victim while I was on the phone.

"Ricardo Jimenez works for a firm that sells restaurant supplies to large resorts such as this one. He visits the island every couple of months but usually only stays for a couple of days. As far as I can tell, he's held his current position for five years."

"So he would be familiar with the island and the staff," I said as a seagull landed on the patio next to my chair. The little buggers had been regular visitors ever since they'd discovered there was a very messy little boy who tended to leave crumbs everywhere staying in the house.

"Looks like," Zak confirmed.

"So any of the staff members on the yacht could have motive to kill him," I concluded.

"It's possible."

"What about the others?" I asked. "Are any of them regulars on the island?"

"Based on lodging records, it appears that both Park and Kim Lee and Charles and Piper Belmont are regular visitors to the island. In fact, it looks like Charles and Piper spend time here almost every year. I didn't find any previous records for Dezi and Lucinda, and I think I remember them saying it was their first visit."

"What about Ricardo's date, Stefana?"

"I didn't find lodging records for anyone by that name. I'd say you were correct in your assumption that she's some type of paid escort. It's very possible the two could have had dates in the past, although they didn't seem to know each other all that well. She could be new to the area."

"So what does this all mean?" I asked.

"At this point it doesn't mean anything, but it's a start, and we both know we have to start somewhere."

I looked out over the calm sea. It was a beautiful afternoon. It seemed crazy to spend it digging into the murder of a man I felt little sympathy for, but I really did want to see the crime solved so I could go home in a week as planned.

"Other than the fact that the man was a regular visitor to the island as well as an abusive dog hater, can we find out anything else about him?" I asked.

"I can find out what brand of toothpaste he favored if you wanted to know that," Zak confirmed.

"I don't think that level of detail will be necessary, but what about phone records during the past few weeks?" I asked.

Zak frowned at the computer. "I can pull up his guest records for the resort. Chances are they'll list a cell phone number. Once I have that, I can dig up a record of his calls, assuming he used a registered phone and not a burner. This is going to take some time. Maybe you want to go get the kids."

"Okay. I could use a walk and I'll take Charlie with me."

It really was the perfect day. I willed myself to relax and enjoy the white sand beach, clear blue sky, aqua water, and close-to-perfect temperature. Maybe we'd go to one of the restaurants that offered outdoor dining that evening. There was going to be a spectacular sunset if the lack of clouds littering the sky was any indication. Once Ellie arrived and could stay with the kids, maybe Zak and I could partake of the moonlit walks I had fantasized about prior to our arrival.

The first thing I noticed when I walked into the Kids Club reception area was a midsized dog sleeping on a dog bed behind the registration counter.

"New dog?" I asked Oria.

"He's a rescue I'm fostering until we can find him a forever home. We don't have a shelter on the island right now, but I'm part of a group that takes strays and abandoned animals into our homes until new families can be identified."

"That's really awesome. I admire your commitment to our four-legged friends."

"It isn't an ideal situation, but we do the best we can with what we have to work with."

"I operate a rescue and rehabilitation shelter where I live," I revealed.

I spent the next fifteen minutes chatting with Oria about the challenges of operating such a facility. I found that the two of us had a lot in common, especially our love of animals. If we lived in the same part of the world, I knew we would be friends.

"There's a fund-raiser for the shelter we're hoping to build this weekend if you're interested," Oria offered.

"I'm very interested. When is it?"

"Saturday evening, on the beach at the far-east end of the island. We usually show an old movie on a giant screen that's really an old sail, and there'll be food and beverages for purchase. After the movie, for those who want to stay, some of the local bands will provide music. We've done similar fund-raisers in the past and they're always a lot of fun. And they're kid friendly if you want to bring Alex and Scooter, although it will be a late evening."

"It sounds awesome. I'll mention it to Zak, but I'm sure he'll be all for it."

"The movie starts as soon as it's dark enough to see the film on the makeshift screen, but most people come early to share a meal and scope out a good spot. If you do make it, look for me and I'll introduce you to some of the other members of the shelter committee. They're a fantastic bunch who really care about the animals on the island."

"I'll do that. Thanks."

I found Scooter and Alex and we headed back to the house, where I hoped Zak had good news. It occurred to me, now that I'd had a chance to think about things, that it was odd that Ricardo had been invited to be a dinner guest on the night of the cruise in the first place. He was simply a vendor for the resort. One of hundreds, most likely. The other guests were all rich businessmen staying in the VIP section of the resort, who were invited to attend with their wives. Ricardo and his escort date didn't seem to fit the profile. As soon as I returned to the house I mentioned that to Zak, who agreed.

"I can ask Jensen about it," Zak said. "I really hadn't stopped to consider that until you mentioned it."

"Did you find anything odd in the phone records?" I asked.

"I'm not sure if it's odd or not, but Ricardo didn't have a cell phone registered, nor had he made any calls from the landline in his room since he'd been here. I suspect he uses a burner phone, which I find odd because he's a salesman. I would think he'd need to have a public number so his clients could reach him."

"Maybe he used a phone owned by and registered to the company he worked for," I suggested.

"Good idea. I'll see what I can find out."

Chapter 5

Thursday, July 30

By the time I got out of bed the next morning Zak had returned from the airport with Ellie. I hugged her like I hadn't seen her for months, even though it had actually only been five days. I'd really hoped that once we got through the wedding things would calm down and level out a bit, but so far that wasn't the way things were turning out for either of us.

"I'm so glad you're here." I squeezed her extra hard. I couldn't imagine the mental turmoil she must be going through.

"Me too. Thanks for encouraging me to come. I feel better already."

"Let's get you settled in and you can catch me up with everything that's going on," I suggested.

"Honestly, I'd much rather focus on your investigation. I'm exhausted from trying to imagine what Levi's new job is going to do to our lives. I could really use a mental vacation from the whole thing."

"Okay, then let's get you settled in and I can catch you up on the investigation."

"Where are the kids?"

"Scooter is hiking with Kids Club and Alex is in her room, working on her book. It seems her parents are going through a rough patch, and while she won't admit it, I can tell it's really affecting her. I think she just needed some alone time."

"I might have something that will cheer her up." Ellie smiled.

I followed Ellie to Alex's room, where she handed the girl a bag. "Phyllis sent these for you."

Alex looked inside and her face lit up like she'd just been given a sackful of puppies.

"What is it?" I asked, assuming correctly that it wasn't puppies.

"Books."

"But I thought you had your Kindle. Isn't it full of books?"

"Yes, but these are special books. When I was FaceTiming with Phyllis the first day we arrived here I mentioned I really wanted to learn more about the history of the island, and she said she'd try to track down some material about this area."

"You FaceTimed with Phyllis?"

"I FaceTime with Phyllis all the time. I've learned so much from her. More than I'll ever learn at the school I've been attending. Not that it was a bad school; it's just that the curriculum is focused on providing a general education for the average student."

Alex's statement sounded like something one of her parents might say. They were trying to get her accepted into a high school for gifted students even though she was only ten. I was worried about her ability to adjust socially if she had to attend classes with students so much older than she was.

"That's great," I said, rather than voicing my concerns. "What did she send?"

Alex showed me each book and explained what she hoped to learn from it. She really did know what information she wanted and seemed to have a good understanding of how to find it.

"Oh, look. This one has information about the church," she gushed.

"The church?" I asked.

"It's the oldest building on the island. It sits atop a bluff you have to hike up to. I really hope we can go see it while we're here."

"It sounds like a fun trip."

"Did you know the entire population of the island was wiped out during a hurricane almost two hundred years ago?" Alex asked.

"Really? I didn't know that."

"I think this volume will have more information about it." Alex opened an old book with yellowed pages and began reading. I could see by the look on her face that she was going to be occupied for the rest of the day, so I led Ellie out to the patio, where Zak was sitting at a table working on his computer.

"Wow, this is beautiful," Ellie gasped.

It really was a gorgeous place to sit and while away the afternoon. Not only were the aqua sea and white sand just beyond the patio wall but there were tropical flowers of a variety of colors growing in pots that decorated the outdoor space.

"So fill me in," Ellie encouraged.

"Let's take a walk while we talk," I suggested. "I'm sure Charlie needs to stretch his legs."

Charlie and I walked down to the beach with Ellie, filling her in on everything Zak and I had discovered. We had a list of suspects, and so far we'd eliminated ourselves; Della, due to her pregnancy;

and Dezi and Lucinda, because they didn't seem to have known Ricardo prior to the dinner cruise. Zak was in the lounge from the time Ricardo disappeared until I found the body. He remembered Stefana had been sitting at the bar, nursing a drink and chatting with the bartender, who we'd identified as Jerrell, during the entire window of death. So we'd eliminated them from the suspect list. Likewise, Kim and Piper were sitting at a table discussing a movie they had both seen during that same window of time, so we'd eliminated them as well. Zak had been speaking to Charles when Jensen offered to show him the bridge. The men had left together but had returned individually. After Charles left with Jensen, Zak entered into a conversation with Park that had lasted until shortly before I found the body. Park had excused himself to use the men's room right before that, and he'd seemed to be away longer than expected, which is why his wife, Kim, went looking for him. She was the one who'd found me kneeling on the floor next to the body.

Based on the approximate time of death and the movement of the people within the lounge, it seemed that Charles, Park, and Jensen were the only ones with opportunity other than myself. Of the identified staff, we assumed Captain Jack was busy steering the boat, but we hadn't actually confirmed that, and we hadn't as of yet established the location of Sebastian, Kai, or Rosa. That left us with seven suspects, as well as the mystery man to whom I'd given the knife.

"This is going to be a lot harder without Salinger to feed us information," Ellie said.

"Yeah," I agreed. "Plus we don't really know any of the suspects, so it isn't going to be easy to just enter into casual conversations like we usually do at home. We need an inside man, especially to show us around and allow us access to the staff who were on board that night."

"Have you met anyone on the island who you might be able to go to for help?" Ellie asked.

"Just Toad, the man I'm required to check in with twice a day. He doesn't strike me as being superknowledgeable about the art of investigation, but he does seem to know about the island. And Talin, the man who interviewed me, seems pretty smart, but I sense it will be hard to get much out of him. In fact, he flat out told me to stay out of it. Zak knows Jensen, but at this point he's still a suspect. Oria, the woman who babysat for the kids while we were at the dinner, runs the Kids Club. She seems really nice and we had a nice conversation yesterday. She's on a committee that's trying to build an animal shelter on the island. By the way, we're invited to attend a fund-raiser on Saturday night. All of us."

"What kind of fund-raiser?" she asked.

I explained about the movie on the beach.

"Sounds like fun."

"Let's head back to see what Zak has found out. Maybe we can wrap this up today and then we can spend the rest of the week on the beach or at the spa."

"It looks like Rosa also works at Kids Club from time to time," Zak offered after we returned. "If I remember correctly, she served the food on the night of the dinner, and her personnel records show that she works part-time in the restaurant and part-time with the kids."

I looked at the clock on the wall. "I know you told Scooter you'd pick him up after lunch. I can go instead and ask Oria about Rosa's schedule. Did you find personnel records for Kai and Sebastian?"

"Sebastian is the head chef in the steak house. He normally works Wednesday through Sunday evenings. The steak house is closed on Mondays and Tuesdays. He was on the yacht on Tuesday, which would have been one of his days off."

"Maybe I can strike up a conversation with Sebastian," Ellie offered. "One chef to another."

"We'll go to the steak house for dinner," I suggested. "What about Kai?"

"Kai's personnel records indicate he works in food services, but they aren't any more specific than that. I'll see if Jensen wants to meet for drinks in the next day or two. Maybe if I can get a few drinks in him he'll spill what he knows about the passengers on the yacht that night. If I remember correctly, he seems to be a talker when he's had a few."

"Great. It looks like we have a plan to at least get started with the staff interviews. As for the guests, any idea how we should approach Charles and Park?" I wondered.

Zak leaned back in his chair and gazed out over the ocean. "Charles and I had begun a conversation regarding a piece of software he was interested in developing when Jensen interrupted to show him the bridge. I could call to invite him and his wife to lunch if Ellie doesn't mind staying with Alex."

"I've been itching to spend some time with a lounger and a good book ever since I walked out onto this beautiful patio," Ellie answered. "You guys go ahead and do the detective thing. Alex and I will stay here and read."

The restaurant where Zak had arranged to meet Charles and Piper was located in the VIP section of the resort, on a cliff overlooking the tall waves that surfers from around the world came to conquer. The red brick patio was lush with the same colorful flowers that grew in the wild within the jungle interior. White tablecloths set with real silver and crystal goblets added elegance to the colorful décor.

Charles and Piper turned out to be entertaining lunch companions once we assured them I'd had nothing to do with the murder on the yacht. They were wonderfully colorful individuals who had traveled the world and had many fascinating stories to tell. I'd never been anywhere until I started dating Zak. To be honest, I'd really never had much of an interest in traveling. Ashton Falls is one of the most beautiful places on earth, and I guess I just couldn't see a reason to go anywhere else. But in the past thirteen months Zak had taken me to Hawaii, Alaska, New York, and now Heavenly Island. He'd opened my eyes to a world I never knew existed.

"So the castle was actually haunted?" I asked with just a slight air of doubt.

"I swear," Piper declared. "When Poppy suggested we vacation in an Irish castle all I could think about was drafty hallways and ancient plumbing, but it turned out to be one of the most fascinating experiences of my life."

I looked at Poppy—Charles—for confirmation that his wife wasn't pulling my leg. He shrugged and smiled. "It's true. The ghost was dim-witted, but the bloke had been six feet under for a good long while."

I really wanted to believe them because how cool would it be to visit a real haunted castle? Still, there was a small part of me that thought this rich and cultured yet slightly nutty couple was teasing me.

"Not everyone who visits the castle sees the ghost," Piper warned. "If I hadn't gotten up to go to the loo I would have missed him entirely. Of course once I knew he was real I got up and looked for him each and every night."

"How was he?" I asked. "I mean, was he scary and mean or more Casperish?"

"He wasn't much to look at, but he seemed harmless," Piper answered. "I can give you the contact information for the castle if you like. Maybe you can talk your Zachary into taking you for a look."

I glanced at Zak.

"I'll take you anywhere you want to go," he said.

"It would be fun to stay in a real castle," I admitted.

"Be sure to request a room in the tower," Charles instructed. "I asked around a bit before we went and learned that the majority of the ghost sightings have occurred on the top floor."

"Do you know who the ghost is supposed to have been?" I asked. I had to admit I was hooked.

"He was the laird of the castle in the late sixteen hundreds," Charles began. "According to the legend, the man kidnapped the daughter of one of the peasants who lived in the village. He kept the girl in the very tower where we stayed. It seems the son of one of his knights fell in love with the girl and vowed to find a way to free her. He convinced some of the villagers to start a fire in order to distract the men guarding the castle, and then he snuck up the back stairway toward the tower. The laird was too smart to fall for such a trick and was waiting for the young man when he arrived. The two men fought and the laird ended up plunging from the balcony to his death on the rocks below."

"And the young man who tried to save the girl?" I asked.

"He was convicted of murdering the laird and beheaded."

"That's an awful story." I frowned.

"Most ghosts are associated with tragic deaths," Piper reminded me.

"Yeah, I guess. What about the girl who'd been kept in the tower?" I asked.

"When the laird died his son took over and ended up falling in love with the girl. They eventually married and had many children. The line was a strong one that has endured. In fact, the current owner of the castle is related to the ghost in some way."

"I guess that part is romantic. It does sound like an awesome adventure."

"If you get over to the UK, pop over to Wales and give us a ring," Piper encouraged. "Poppy just loves to give visitors the grand tour. Don't you, dear?"

"I have to admit that part of me has always felt I should have been a tour guide rather than a businessman."

At this point the conversation drifted to business opportunities in the UK and I tuned out. Hearing Piper's tales of world travel had been both entertaining and fascinating, but listening to a discussion about economic trends was downright tiresome. I'd really been enchanted by the story of the ghost of the castle and the legacy he left. If life settled down a bit and the opportunity afforded itself, I very much wanted to make a trip to the Emerald Isle.

"Jensen seems to be interested in the same general idea," Zak said, bringing the conversation around to the island and the people we were there to investigate.

"Yes, we've engaged in several discussions regarding the idea." Charles nodded.

"So you've been to the island before?" Zak asked, even though he already knew the answer to the question.

"On many occasions. Jensen and I go way back. Since before he built the resort. Piper and I visit the island every year or two so we can catch up. His wife, Della, went to Oxford with my younger sister."

"Really?" Zak said. "When Jensen offered to show you the bridge I just assumed it was your first time on the yacht."

"It was my first time on *that* yacht," Charles responded. "That one is a new addition to his fleet. We haven't been here in over a year."

"I wish I'd asked for a tour," I commented. "I would have liked to meet Captain Jack. I hear he's an interesting man."

"The bloke is nothing more than a salty old sailor. I'm not sure why Jensen keeps him on staff. I imagine they have a history of some sort."

"Does it take more than one person to pilot a yacht of that size?" I asked.

"No. It's mostly computerized."

"I see." I tried to appear both interested and uninformed. "When you visited the bridge did you happen to see any of the other guests or crew?"

"Trying to figure out who might have whacked our philandering salesman?"

"Given the fact that I seem to be the prime suspect, I'd like to figure out who really did it," I answered honestly.

"I'm afraid that other than Jack, I didn't see anyone lingering about," Charles answered.

"I suppose you must have known Ricardo before the cruise if you've visited the island often," I fished.

"I don't know him well, but I was introduced to him on one occasion by a shared acquaintance who later warned me that the man was heavily invested in seedy activities, so I would be best served to avoid him. I was actually surprised Jensen invited him to join us the other evening. He normally reserves invitations on his yacht for his most important guests."

"And the shared acquaintance?"

"A delightful woman named Chandella. She works as some sort of executive assistant to Jensen and has attended quite a few social gatherings as Jensen's guest when his Della wasn't available."

The conversation paused as the waiter took away our salad plates and replaced them with the main course. I'd ordered baked salmon over arugula.

"This looks delicious," I commented. I wanted to say something about the true nature of Chandella's job, according to Talin, but decided to let it go. "I know the chef who worked the dinner cruise normally works at the steak house near the beach. Do you happen to know who's responsible for this wonderful creation?"

"I do." Charles smiled proudly. "His name is Jimbo. I can introduce you, if you'd like."

"I hate to bother him if he's busy."

"Nonsense. Jimbo loves it when people fuss over his food." Charles waved the waiter over and asked him to request an audience with the chef. The man nodded and headed toward the kitchen.

I almost spit my wine directly into Charles's smiling face when the dark-skinned man I'd seen on the yacht walked through the dining room and out onto the patio.

Chapter 6

"Are you sure it was the same man?" Ellie asked a couple of hours later. We were sitting on loungers at the pool, watching Scooter and Alex splash around.

"I'm sure."

"But you said he in no way indicated that he recognized you."

"Maybe he was just covering. If he killed Ricardo, he wouldn't want to draw attention to the fact that he was on the yacht the night of the murder."

"What does Zak think?" Ellie asked.

"He said there was no indication the man recognized me. He's certain I'm remembering the whole thing wrong. Still, he did say he'd try to find out where Jimbo was at the time of the cruise."

I waved to Scooter, who was yelling to me to watch him while he did a cannonball into the water. The ensuing splash created quite the frenzy when a huge wave covered a pair of teenage girls who were sunbathing. After explaining to Scooter that cannonballs were best saved for our private pool at home, I returned to Ellie and our conversation.

"If we have a chance to speak to Sebastian when we go to dinner tonight, let's find a way to ask him if Jimbo was on the yacht that night. If he *was* there he must have been in the kitchen."

"I thought you said Zak said every single person on board was interviewed when they disembarked," Ellie reminded me.

"He did say that." I found I was growing both irritated and frustrated. "But I also know what I saw. If I imagined the guy with the knife, what are the chances I'd imagine a guy who looked exactly like a real person living on the island?"

"Maybe you'd seen Jimbo before and your mind filled in the blanks."

"That isn't what happened," I snapped.

Ellie looked hurt by my sharp tone.

"I'm sorry. I don't know why I'm taking this out on you. You're just trying to help. I guess I just feel so frustrated that I saw a man everyone keeps telling me I couldn't have seen. I don't know how he got on the boat or where he went after I spoke to him in the hall, but I do know what I saw. The thing is, I have absolutely no way to prove Jimbo was on the yacht the night of the murder."

Ellie squeezed my hand. "I believe you. I really do. If Jimbo was on the yacht we'll figure out a way to prove it."

"He wasn't on the yacht." Zak walked up from behind us while we were talking. He sat down in the lounger next to mine.

"What do you mean, he wasn't on the yacht? I saw him."

"On the night of the murder he worked in the restaurant where we had lunch. I spoke to three different staff members who all verified that he was there until closing. There was no way you could have seen him."

I let out a long breath. Maybe I really was losing my mind.

"Is there any possibility that the staff is just covering for Jimbo?" I asked.

"I guess there is a possibility, but I kind of doubt it. Besides, Jensen keeps a close eye on his staff, especially the ones who work in the VIP area of the resort. If you're that sure you saw Jimbo on the yacht I guess I could access his employee record."

"I'd appreciate that," I answered. "As for the other staff, I spoke to Oria when I picked Scooter up. She confirmed that Rosa does work at Kids Club part-time, but she hadn't seen her for a couple of weeks. It seems they've been shorthanded in food services so she's been concentrating her hours there. She did say Rosa's helped out with dinner cruises in the past. I asked whether she thought Rosa might know Ricardo, and she confirmed that because he sold restaurant supplies almost everyone in food services would know him to some degree, but she didn't think they were all that well acquainted."

"I guess we leave her on the list," Zak said.

"Did you have a chance to ask Jensen about drinks?"

"I called his office and left a message, but he hasn't gotten back to me. I'm sure he will. In the meantime, how about a swim in the ocean?"

"The kids seem happy in the pool," I pointed out.

"I can watch them," Ellie offered. "In fact, take your time and enjoy a few hours to yourselves. This is, after all, your honeymoon."

I'm happy to say Zak and I made *very* good use of our time alone.

Later that evening, the five of us went to dinner in the steak house as planned. The further we dove into the facts surrounding Ricardo Jimenez's death, though, the more terrified I became that I actually *had* killed the man. I'd been furious with the jerk and I *had* gone to the kitchen to fetch the knife. Maybe I really had plunged the knife into his back, causing my mind to supply an alternate killer who really wasn't there.

Of course that was nuts. I wouldn't really kill someone, no matter how mad I was at them, and I certainly wouldn't forget doing so if I had. The only explanation was that someone had killed Ricardo between the time I'd returned the knife to the man in black and the time I found his body in the hallway. It did seem odd that no one had heard anything. Sure, the group in the lounge had been talking to one another, creating a certain level of noise, and there had been soft music playing in the background, but still, if someone stabbed me in the back I'm sure I'd get off a good loud scream before I died. At the very least there should have been the sound of a scuffle.

Unless . . .

I let myself consider all the possibilities. Suppose someone could have snuck up on Ricardo from behind and placed a hand over his mouth before plunging the knife in his back. For that to occur, the person who did the stabbing would have needed to be both tall and strong. The killer could have used an aid to immobilize the man prior to stabbing him, like chloroform.

I wondered about the knife that had been used. Yes, I'd gotten my fingerprints all over it when I'd removed the knife from the man's back in an effort to perform CPR, but could anyone else's fingerprints be on it as well? I wondered if Talin would be willing to share information if I asked him nicely. I realized he didn't know me the way Salinger did, but we'd come to an understanding of sorts during my interview on Tuesday.

"Is something wrong with your food?" Alex asked.

I realized all I'd done since the main course had been served was push it around on my plate.

"No, but Zak and I had a big lunch. I guess I never had the chance to burn it off. How's your scampi?"

"It's really good. Do you want to try a bite?"

"Thanks, but I think I'll pass this evening. Maybe another time."

"I'll share my hamburger with you if you want," Scooter offered.

I smiled at the ten-year-old with ketchup all over his face. "Thanks, but I'm not really hungry. How was Kids Camp today?"

Scooter proceeded to fill the silence with a solid ten minutes of very detailed descriptions as to how really awesome Kids Camp had been. Ellie had been trying all evening to cheer me up, but she seemed to have given up. Zak was a lot more quiet than usual. The only conclusion I could come to was that even he was beginning to suspect I was guilty of murdering Ricardo Jimenez.

"It's going to be okay," Ellie whispered to me when I failed to laugh at Scooter's joke.

"Maybe it will and maybe it won't," I whispered back as Scooter continued with his story. "I've gone over the scenario in the hallway in my mind a million times. I know what I saw, but every single piece of evidence seems to counter that memory."

"Memories are tricky things," Ellie sympathized. "Especially during stressful situations."

Zak, Ellie, and Alex all laughed at Scooter's story and I laughed as well, even though I had no idea what he'd just said. There was a voice in my head telling me to go back over things again to try to figure out anything I might have missed.

I'd gone to the kitchen to find a knife for the cake. The room was empty. The dishes were done and the food had been put away. I remember that Jerrell was still at the bar, but I have no idea where Sebastian, Kai, and Rosa had gone off to. In a way, it was odd that they weren't hanging around just in case someone needed something from the kitchen. I remember seeing the knife on the counter. I walked over and picked it up and then started back toward the lounge, where the others were waiting. It was at that point that the dark-skinned man in black clothing, who I was certain looked exactly like Jimbo, intercepted me. He told me that I had the wrong knife. He then took the knife from me and assured me he'd bring the right one. I'd continued on to the lounge.

If no one in the lounge had seen him, he couldn't have come from there to the kitchen, so where *had* he come from? I tried to picture the hallway. There weren't any intersections in it, so there must have been a door to another room that I hadn't noticed.

Suddenly, I knew I needed to get another look at the interior of the yacht. I just needed a way to score an invitation.

"Sebastian will see you now," the waiter informed me. "He thought you might want to see the kitchen, so he suggested he'd speak with you there."

When we'd first arrived I'd asked for an audience for Ellie and me on the pretext that she was a well-known chef in Ashton Falls. I suppose the whole chef thing might have been a stretch, but Ellie was the best cook I knew and I was certain she could hold her own in a conversation with Sebastian.

"Thank you." I looked at Ellie. "Are you ready?"

"I am." She put her napkin down on the table next to her mostly empty plate.

Ellie and I followed the waiter through the restaurant to the immaculate kitchen. I could tell by the look on her face that Ellie was in awe. Not only was the room large and modern, with state-of-the-art appliances, but the five men who were working with Sebastian were going about their tasks with a precision that was truly amazing.

"Wow," Ellie finally managed to utter. "Your kitchen is amazing."

"Thank you. I designed it myself when the restaurant was built almost fifteen years ago."

"So you've been here almost from the beginning," I commented.

"Almost. The resort currently has five restaurants and this was the third one to be built." Sebastian turned to Ellie. "So you are a chef in your hometown."

I watched the hustle and bustle of waiters coming in and out to gather plates filled with fabulous-looking food that the kitchen staff had assembled with admirable efficiency. I knew the chitchat portion of the conversation was necessary, but I really hoped Ellie would get around to asking about the yacht. Rosa, Jerrell, Kai, and Sebastian all had attended the dinner cruise as part of the culinary staff. Other than Captain Jack, they really did make the best suspects.

"By the way, the dinner you prepared the other night was to die for," I interrupted. "I do hope you had a chance to have some?"

"The kitchen staff and I ate in the lounge on the bottom deck while the guests were all on the upper deck after dinner," Sebastian confirmed. "I must say I really did outdo myself with the stuffed lobster."

"That must be why no one was in the kitchen when I went in there to look for a knife," I commented.

"Jerrell remained on the upper deck in the event that anyone needed something. You should have asked him to fetch a knife if you needed one," Sebastian scolded.

"Yes, in retrospect that's what I should have done. I just figured I'd find Rosa or Kai in the kitchen because they'd done such a fantastic job of taking care of our needs up to that point."

Sebastian looked at me oddly. I suppose my statement could have come off sounding like a complaint, although I was actually just fishing for additional information on the movement of the kitchen staff.

"Yes, the pair do a good job," Sebastian eventually replied.

"It must be quite a challenge to cook for a large group on the yacht when you're used to the spaciousness of this facility," Ellie commented.

"Not really. The number of guests I must feed during a dinner cruise does not even compare to the number I serve in the restaurant each evening."

"I'm sorry I missed the cruise." Ellie sighed. "I would love to have seen the kitchen on the vessel.

There's something very romantic about the notion of cooking at sea."

Was Ellie flirting?

"I'd be happy to show you the kitchen any time you'd like," Sebastian offered. "We wouldn't be able to actually take the boat out without Captain Jack in attendance, but I'm sure Mr. Ewing won't mind if I gave you a tour. I'd need to clear it with him first of course, but I don't anticipate a problem."

I nodded at Ellie to accept. This might provide me with the opportunity I needed to sneak around and figure out how the man I know I saw did what he did.

"Would tomorrow work?" Ellie asked.

"Say eleven thirty?" Sebastian confirmed.

"I'll meet you there."

Ellie and Sebastian chatted for a few more minutes before he waved the waiter over to take us back to our table.

"Way to go, Ellie," I complimented once we'd returned to our table.

"How'd it go?" Zak asked.

"Ellie flirted her way into an invitation to take a tour of the yacht," I answered.

"I wasn't flirting. I really am interested."

"You were flirting," I insisted. "And it worked. I really think I can figure this out if I can take a look around. I especially want to get a look at the lower level of the yacht. If there was a dark-skinned man on board, and there was, he must have been hiding below the main deck where we spent the majority of the evening."

"Sebastian didn't exactly invite you to come along," Ellie reminded me.

"So I'll just show up. What is he going to do? I'll excuse myself to use the ladies' room while he shows you the kitchen. I won't need long. All I need to figure out at this point is how the man I saw could have gotten into the hallway without going through either the kitchen or the lounge, and where he might have gone after he killed Ricardo Jimenez."

Chapter 7

Friday, July 31

I decided it would be in my best interest to feed Toad a small amount of information so it wouldn't look like I was keeping things from him. It would be easy for him to find out that Zak and I had dined with Charles and Piper, so it made sense that I would bring this up to him before he could ask me about it. I'd also decided to let him know I'd visited the yacht with Ellie after our visit. I didn't want him to hear about it from someone else, but I also didn't want him to try to stop me from going.

"Morning, Toad," I greeted him as I entered the small, dingy office.

"You are early today."

"I have a busy day planned with my family and wanted to be sure to have my mandatory check-in before things got too hectic. I don't suppose you have any news?"

"Nothing new."

"In the spirit of full disclosure, I want to tell you that Zak and I had lunch with Charles and Piper Belmont yesterday. I wasn't snooping," I quickly assured him. "Zak and Charles had business to discuss and I decided to tag along. Did you know the couple have visited a real haunted castle?"

Toad looked skeptical.

"Charles did mention that he'd been introduced to Ricardo by Chandella, who warned him to stay away from the guy. He didn't say when this introduction occurred, but I guess it was during one of his previous visits to the island. His comment got me wondering about Chandella. Talin indicated that she's Jensen Ewing's mistress, yet Charles stated that he believed she was some sort of an executive assistant. He said she'd attended social engagements with him in Della's absence."

"So?" Toad shrugged.

"Do you think Della knows about Jensen and Chandella?"

"I'm sure she does."

"And she doesn't mind that her husband is cheating on her?"

Toad snickered. "Mr. Ewing isn't cheating. Men in this country frequently take mistresses if they can afford to do so. This does not diminish Mrs. Ewing's role as Mr. Ewing's wife. Do you have anything else to report?"

"No. That's it for now. I'll see you this evening. Oh, I forgot to mention that Zak and I have been invited to a fund-raiser on Saturday for the animal shelter. I assume there's no problem with our attending?"

Toad shrugged again. "I don't see a problem, as long as you are there to watch the movie and not interrogate the other suspects."

"So you do think there are other suspects?" I smiled.

"Perhaps."

After completing my conversation with Toad I headed back to the house. Alex and Scooter were going to spend the morning at Kids Club and Zak planned to go surfing while Ellie and I met with Chef Sebastian on the yacht. If I could figure out how someone might have accessed the hallway undetected, maybe I could finally convince Zak and Talin that someone really had been in the hallway that night.

Ellie and I arrived at the yacht at exactly eleven thirty. I could tell Sebastian was less than thrilled to see me, but I had to give him credit; he didn't say anything about my presence and was quite gracious in his attempt to include both Ellie and me in the conversation. I felt a little bad when I realized he'd brought lunch for Ellic and himself, but rather than point out the fact that my presence was an obvious intrusion, he simply divided the meal between the three of us.

Ellie and Sebastian did seem to have a lot to talk about. I understood that it was important for her to show interest in all the special gadgets that were required to prepare a meal at sea, but I really was more interested in access points to the hallway than I was the spice rack that Sebastian had contracted to be specially built for the kitchen.

"Would you like to see the rest of the yacht?" Sebastian finally asked after a long conversation about the challenges of cooking when the sea was rough.

"I'd love to." Ellie grinned. "Zoe?"

"I guess a tour would be fun." I tried to appear nonchalant.

"Why don't we start at the top and work our way down?" Sebastian suggested.

I'd already seen the top deck and was more interested in the lower two but didn't say as much. I did learn during the tour that there was an exterior stairway on the port side that allowed a person to move between decks without accessing the interior stairway we all had used the night of the dinner. That fact alone seemed worth the long and boring conversation I'd just endured.

Luckily, the tour of the top deck went quickly, so it was only a short wait before we went down to the main deck, where we'd been entertained on the night of the dinner. As I suspected, the hallway where I'd found Ricardo's body provided access to the stairway leading to the bottom deck, where the bedrooms were located. There was a sliding door veiling the staircase, which is why I hadn't noticed it on the night of the cruise. I realized this was the staircase Sebastian and the other staff members must have used when they headed down to have their dinner. I asked him if he'd seen a man in black on the lower deck that evening and he said he hadn't.

The most interesting thing I found out about the 150-foot yacht was that not only did it feature a helicopter pad but it also had a docking bay that held two WaveRunners. As I considered the fact that one of the two WaveRunners was missing, I suddenly knew how my mystery man had left the boat. Now all I had to do was prove it.

Zak was back from surfing by the time we got back to the house. Ellie offered to pick up the kids from Kids Club and then spend the afternoon with them so Zak and I could have a little alone time. There was a marina near the house that rented sailboats by the hour, so we packed a hamper with champagne and fruit, cheese, and crackers and set off for a trip to a secret cove Zak had heard about from some of the local surfers.

It was a beautiful day, with just enough of a breeze to power the small boat without it being so windy as to feel overpowering. As it had been every day since we'd arrived, the sky was a deep blue that matched the sea almost exactly. The local gossip line still spoke of a storm on the horizon. Based on the chatter we'd overheard, it sounded like we could expect the arrival of wind and rain at some point on Sunday. Oria had warned me that these storms tended to come on all of a sudden, so it was best to count more on the accuracy of the weather report than the current conditions.

When we got to the cove where Zak was headed we found a small, isolated beach that was completely deserted. We anchored just offshore and then, placing our food hamper, towels, and other supplies on a rubber raft, swam from the boat to the shore.

"Now this is the life," I commented as I stretched out on the blanket we'd brought and let the warm sun caress my back and shoulders.

"I'll admit this is closer to the honeymoon I imagined than most of this trip has been."

"Oh, I don't know. The hike to the waterfall was pretty special." I grinned.

Zak leaned over and kissed my shoulder. "I guess we've done okay. Not that I want to break the mood, but how was your trip to the yacht?"

I filled him in on what I'd discovered, including the fact that a WaveRunner was missing.

"I had no idea the yacht was outfitted with personal watercraft. Maybe someone did sneak in before the boat sailed, hid out belowdecks, killed Ricardo, and then grabbed a WaveRunner to make a getaway."

"I told you I wasn't imagining things."

"I should know by now never to doubt you."

I rolled over and looked around at the deserted beach. "I suppose there might be a way you can make it up to me."

Zak leaned over and kissed me. "Yeah? What exactly did you have in mind?"

By the time we'd returned to the boat and headed back to the marina the wind had all but died. It was obvious the trip back was going to take a lot longer than the one to the cove.

"Did Jensen ever get back to you?" I asked Zak.

He nodded. "I'm supposed to meet him in the bar at six thirty." He looked at his watch. "Maybe we should have headed back sooner."

"I think the wind will shift once we get around the point," I said. "Are you joining us for dinner?"

"Yeah. I told Jensen I wanted to buy him a drink to thank him for allowing us to use the house, but I planned to slip in the few questions we'd discussed and be back to the house for a late dinner. Maybe we can just BBQ on the patio."

"I'll stop to get some supplies after I check in with Toad," I offered. "I think the kids would enjoy a casual dinner after all the nights we've made them clean up at the end of the day."

"They seem to be having a good time," Zak observed.

"Yeah, they are. I wish I didn't have this murder investigation to deal with. I hoped we'd all have more time to spend together. I'm going to miss them when they go back to school. I wonder if Alex's parents ever heard back from that high school they were trying to get her in to."

"I've been thinking a lot about the upcoming school year," Zak informed me. "I know you're concerned that Alex won't fit in if she boards at a high school, and I agree. I also agree with her parents that she's outgrown her current school scholastically."

"It's a difficult situation." I sighed. "I understand that it would be a waste to leave her where she is, but I want her to have a normal childhood, or at least as normal as a ten-year-old genius can."

"I've been thinking about things since you first brought up the situation. I have an idea how we could open the school for a limited number of students this fall."

"So we're really going to do this? The school?"

"I thought it was what you wanted."

"It is. It's just all happening so fast."

"If we want to have a facility built in a year, we'll need to move fast. If you're having second thoughts, now would be the time to voice them."

"No," I decided. "No second thoughts. I'm excited about having Scooter and Alex nearby, and when we decide to have our own little Zimmermans, a school nearby will be a perfect solution for them as well. What's your idea for Alex for this year?"

"There are actually three minors we're interested in educating: Alex, who needs a specialized education to meet the needs of her advanced rate of learning in pretty much every area; Scooter, who possesses average intelligence and would do fine in any elementary school but needs a stable living situation in order to thrive; and Pi, who's suffering academically overall mainly due to his reluctance to attend classes but possesses a brilliant mind when it comes to understanding and being able to manipulate various forms of technology. Like Scooter, Pi needs a stable living environment."

"How's your request to become Pi's guardian coming along?" I asked.

"I still haven't heard back, but I don't see a problem with the request being approved—unless, of course, my new wife is actually convicted of murder."

I glared at Zak.

"In any event, the development of Zimmerman Academy seems to be the answer to all these challenges over the long run. The problem we face now has to do with finding a solution to the educational needs of these three individuals for the upcoming school year."

"And?" I knew Zak must have figured something out or we wouldn't be having this discussion, although he seemed to be taking the long way around to get to the point.

"I spoke to Phyllis about the situation with Alex. She agrees with us that the girl has special needs. She told me she'd be willing to homeschool Alex if we were to have her come live with us."

"I'd be happy to have her live with us."

"I figured as much. However, the conversation brought us around to providing Alex with a broad education that would encompass all her needs. Phyllis pointed out that Alex would benefit socially from attending school with her peers, although she agrees that if she were to attend middle school she might not be challenged academically."

"And you've come up with a solution?"

"Perhaps. Our idea is to have Alex attend middle school half a day. Yes, she'll still be the youngest student at the school, but a ten-year-old attending classes with twelve- and thirteen-year-olds is much preferable to attending classes with fourteen- to eighteen-year-olds."

"You said she'd go to the middle school for only half a day?"

"Phyllis and I and maybe a few others would work with her in the afternoons to make sure she's as challenged academically as she deserves."

I hugged Zak. "It sounds like a perfect solution. Have you spoken to Alex's parents about it?"

"Not yet. I wanted to run it past you first. I mean, we *are* a newly married couple, and I wasn't sure how you'd feel about having a houseful of kids right away."

"Houseful?" I asked.

"I just figured that as long as we had this awesome teaching team on board, we could have Scooter and Pi move in with us as well. Scooter will do fine at the elementary school, and we talked about using the same half-day option with Pi at the high school that we discussed for Alex."

Alex was a perfectly behaved angel who in many ways was more mature than I was. Scooter could be a handful, but Zak seemed to be able to handle him. But Pi? Pi was a teenage dropout with behavior issues. Was I really ready to take that on?

"You're worried about Pi," Zak stated.

"It's just that he's sixteen. Are we ready to take on a teenager?"

"I'll admit he could very well turn out to be a huge challenge, but I feel like he really needs us. He's worth saving."

I took a deep breath. "Okay. Let's do this."

Zak pulled me into his arms. "Have I told you lately how much I love you?"

"Yes. But I wouldn't mind hearing it again."

"Well, I do. Love you. And there's more."

"More?"

"Phyllis had agreed to take on the scheduling of all the Ashton Falls residents who have agreed to participate. It occurred to me that if we're going to have access to the talents of this amazing group of people, maybe we should open the afternoon program to a few others."

"You want to have other kids move in with us?"

"No, not that. I thought about asking Abby if she'd be interested in participating. She's a bright girl who would benefit from an accelerated education, but she has a home. Hazel mentioned a couple of other local children who she felt would benefit likewise. Phyllis said she has a friend who's concerned about her niece, who is bright but has had some behavior issues and was kicked out of the private school she attended last year. She hasn't personally met the niece, but she spoke to the friend, who indicated that she believed the girl would do wonderfully in such an environment. Phyllis indicated that she was willing to have her move in with her if her parents were on board. As you know, Phyllis has a large home and has volunteered to allow a couple of other girls to stay with her if we identified additional students who needed to board. We discussed starting out with about ten students who would normally be in the seventh to tenth grades."

"You've really thought this through."

"I have."

I looked at Zak in awe. "I brought up the idea for the Zimmerman Academy less than two weeks ago. We've gotten married and solved a murder in the meantime. How have you had time to arrange all this?"

Zak shrugged. "I'm efficient."

As we rounded the point the wind picked up, as I'd predicted it would, so our conversation was stalled while Zak committed his attention to sailing the boat. Zak did manage to inform me that there was a building in town he hoped to rent to house the temporary academy, but if that didn't work out, my parents had offered to allow him to modify their pool house, which was no longer in use, to serve as our temporary school. When had Zak had time to talk to my parents?

Chapter 8

"I almost gave up on you," Toad said when I checked in with him later than usual. I had to wonder about the specifics of Toad's job. No matter what time of day I popped in, I found him sitting in a rickety old chair with his feet propped up on a desk covered with dusty files. Did the man never move? And if he was supposed to be investigating Ricardo Jimenez's murder wouldn't you think he'd need to go outside and talk to people at some point? The entire situation was extremely odd.

"I told you I had a busy day," I reminded him. "But I'm here now and I have news. I don't suppose Talin is around?"

"Nope. It's just me. So what is your news?"

I really had hoped Talin would be in. He at least seemed more likely to do something with the information I had uncovered. As odd as it was that Toad never seemed to leave the building, Talin never seemed to be around. I hadn't seen him again since the night of the murder and the interview.

"Did Talin tell you that I suspect the man I saw in the hallway who took the knife from me is actually the killer?" I asked.

"The man who wasn't on the boat," Toad stated with a voice filled with sarcastic disbelief.

"The man who was *on the boat*," I corrected. "I found out today that the yacht carries two personal watercraft belowdecks. My friend Ellie was invited to have lunch on the yacht and I decided to tag along.

While I was there I found out that one of the two WaveRunners is missing."

"You just happened to score an invitation to have lunch on the yacht?" Toad looked at me skeptically.

"Ellie just happened to score the invite," I told him. "I simply tagged along. Ellie is a chef back home and Chef Sebastian seems to have a thing for her. So what do you think?"

"About Sebastian and your friend?"

"No. About the missing WaveRunner. Isn't it possible that the man I saw in the hallway that night snuck on board before we all boarded, hid downstairs, killed Ricardo, and then made his getaway while everyone was in a panic over the dead body?"

Toad seemed to be considering my theory. "Yeah, I guess it could have happened that way. I'll talk to Talin about this new information when I see him next."

"Thanks. It would be nice not to be the only suspect in this convoluted case."

"Don't worry. Talin and I have been doing more than sitting around on our backsides. We are now up to three solid suspects, and that was before you provided this theory as to how your mystery man could have pulled off what you believe he did."

"Three?" I asked, thrilled to no longer be alone in this particular category. "Who are the other two?"

"I'm afraid I really can't say."

"Come on, Toad. You know I didn't do it. Throw me a bone; at least give me a small hope that I'm not going to rot in your disgusting jail."

Toad just smiled. I could see he wasn't going to just spill the news without some sort of motivation. I wished I'd had the foresight to bring money, but the grocery took resort cash, so I hadn't had a need for the real stuff.

"It has to be someone on the yacht that night," I concluded.

Zak and I had narrowed it down to Charles, Park, and Jensen, assuming that Sebastian hadn't been lying about the staff being together. Of course there was Captain Jack. He'd been piloting the boat, but I suppose he could have snuck away for a few minutes.

"One of the suspects must be Park." I watched Toad's face. He definitely didn't have a poker face, so I knew I was right. "Park left to go to the bathroom and was gone during the entire window of death. In fact, the reason Kim found me with the body was because she decided to go look for him. I don't suppose you might know why Park would have wanted Ricardo dead?"

Toad just raised an eyebrow over one beady eye.

"As for suspect number two, I'm going to go with Captain Jack."

Bingo. I could tell by the huge effort Toad went to not to have an expression on his face that I'd hit it on the head.

"I know Captain Jack and Ricardo knew each other because I saw them talking on the beach. I also suspected Captain Jack was the first person on board that night, so he could have made whatever arrangements he needed to, including sneaking my mystery man aboard before anyone else got there. He was piloting the boat, but I've learned that the vessel is computerized, so he could have set the autopilot, killed Ricardo, and then returned to the bridge before anyone knew he was gone."

"You seem to have thought about this quite a lot," Toad observed.

"Of course I've thought about it. My freedom is at stake. Keep in mind that Talin said I shouldn't investigate. He never said I couldn't think about it. Are you going to the fund-raiser tomorrow?"

Toad seemed startled by my abrupt change of subject.

"Yes, I planned to. Why do you ask?"

"It just seemed like a good place to trip over information. If you're there and I happen to trip over something important I won't have to wait to fill you in."

Toad actually chuckled. "You have a strange logic, Zoe Donovan."

"So I've been told."

After I finished talking to Toad I decided to call Jeremy to see how the new dogs were working out. I knew he would do everything in his power to make certain we were able to accommodate as many of the poor things as possible.

"So how's it going?" I asked as soon as he answered the phone and we dispensed with the traditional pleasantries.

"Really good. Your idea about asking locals to help foster the dogs was brilliant. Not only did we take on the fifteen dogs we had room for at the Zoo but I had seven members of the community volunteer to foster one or more dogs. In addition to Nick, who agreed to foster three females with health issues, your pappy took on two mama dogs with active litters, and Tiffany took three pregnant females back to your house. I hope that's okay."

"That's more than okay; that's awesome. And Nick's a retired doctor, so he was a good choice for the injured dogs. Has Scott had a chance to check all of them out?"

Scott Walden is our local veterinarian.

"He's working on it. So far he's cleared about half of the dogs for adoption and is going to work on spreading the word that we're in need of qualified adoptive families."

"That's one of the reasons I love Ashton Falls so much. When there's a need, the entire community pitches in to meet it."

"Yeah. It's a pretty awesome place to live. I think we might want to extend the adoption clinic we've planned from one day to two now that we have a full house."

"That's a good idea. Go ahead and change the ad, and put a notice in the Bryton Lake paper as well. We're going to need to lure folks up the mountain if we're going to place that many animals."

Later that evening, after we'd BBQ'd burgers and shared a meal with Ellie and the kids, Zak, Charlie, and I decided to take a walk on the beach. It was a moonless night and the stars shone brightly in the dark sky. The tide was out, causing the waves to lap gently onto the shore.

"So how did your conversation with Jensen go?" I asked. I really wished Zak and I could be spending more of our time together as a newly married couple rather than focusing all of our energy on murder and motives, but we were scheduled to fly home in just five days and I really wanted to be allowed to leave the island when the time came.

"He was actually quite helpful," Zak informed me. "The man really doesn't hold his liquor well. It only took two drinks and he was blabbing anything and everything."

"What did he say about Ricardo specifically?"

"I asked about his presence on the cruise, and he said Ricardo and Stefana were last-minute additions to the group due to a request from Chandella that they be included."

"Did he know why Chandella asked?" I remembered Ricardo pulling her into the breezeway on the morning of the dinner cruise. Chances were that was when he was arranging for the invitation.

"He said she owed him a favor and he'd asked her to arrange for his invitation. He also verified that Stefana works for Chandella as an escort. According to Jensen, they hadn't met prior to Chandella arranging for Stefana to accompany Ricardo on the cruise."

"So I guess the million-dollar question is, why did Ricardo want to go on the cruise? We can't ask him, but maybe Chandella knows. I'll see if I can just happen to run into her tomorrow."

Zak took my hand in his. "Please be careful. You're supposed to stay away from the investigation. I don't want you to end up back in jail."

"I'll be careful. In fact, I'll fill Toad in before I track down Chandella. Maybe he'll want to ask her about Ricardo himself. I just want this murder solved; I really don't care who solves it."

I watched as Charlie chased the waves as the water receded and then flowed back onto the beach. He was certainly having fun on this trip. He loved the fact that Scooter and Alex were there to play with him. It made me happy to see him having such a good time.

"Did Jensen say anything else that might prove to be helpful?" I eventually asked.

"No, but I did find out something interesting. I decided to run a check on Ricardo's finances while I was waiting for you to get back from town, and I found an offshore account with five deposits into it for twenty thousand dollars each. The entire balance of the account was transferred out the day after the cruise. I haven't had a chance to trace the source of the deposits, but I'm going to."

"That's a lot of money. It's interesting that the money was transferred out the day after the man died."

"I thought so as well, although the transfer would have had to have been initiated before his death."

"I don't follow."

"There's a forty-eight-hour holding period between the time a transfer is initiated and completed. The transfer was completed the morning after he died, which means it would have been initiated the morning of the day before he died."

"That seems relevant," I pointed out.

"Yeah, I thought so too. I'm working on tracking down both the source of the deposits into the account and the destination of the deposits out."

"Hopefully, the information will help us to nail Ricardo's killer. Do you think Talin will really prevent me from leaving the island if the case isn't resolved by Wednesday?" I asked.

Zak squeezed my hand. "I don't know. What I do know is that I'm not leaving without you. If Talin won't allow you to go, I'll arrange for Coop to come for Ellie and the kids. Let's just hope it doesn't come to that."

I leaned my head against Zak's shoulder as we walked. God, I loved this man. I'd managed to make a mess of our honeymoon due to my impulsive behavior, but he didn't seem mad in the least. I vowed at that moment to find a way to show him just how much he meant to me.

"I almost forgot to tell you that I'm no longer the only suspect in the case," I informed Zak. "When I checked in with Toad he indicated that they were up to three. He wouldn't say who the other two were, but when I speculated that both Park and Captain Jack might be suspects his expression told me that I'd guessed correctly."

"Neither of the two men have alibis," Zak confirmed. "Maybe I should dig around in their backgrounds a bit. Park was out of the room when Ricardo was stabbed. He seems a likely suspect. If we can discover how they're connected maybe we can figure out a motive."

"Now that I think about it, Park is the one who requested that the remainder of the cake be cut. He's the one who sent me to the kitchen for the knife. I wonder if he was intentionally trying to set me up."

Zak frowned. "Why would he do that?"

"Because of all the people on board the yacht that night I was the easiest to frame. Everyone had witnessed my argument with Ricardo."

I stopped to consider the idea further. "What if Park was working with the man in black? He sent me to the kitchen to fetch the knife. I picked it up, ensuring that my fingerprints were all over it. Even if Kim hadn't found me kneeling next to the body, I would probably be a suspect once they dusted for prints. Park disappeared when I went to the kitchen the first time. If we assume he didn't really go to the men's room I wonder where he went."

"Ricardo was missing from the room as well," Zak pointed out. "Maybe the men arranged to meet while everyone else was in the lounge."

"The question is, where did they meet and how did Ricardo end up dead in the hallway? I wonder if Kim was in on it. The timing of her deciding to look for Park couldn't have worked out better."

"The question I keep coming back to is, why the yacht?" Zak asked. "If the whole thing was an elaborate setup, why kill Ricardo on the boat, where there were limited suspects? It would make more sense to simply ambush him on the beach or in his room."

"Yeah," I agreed. "You do have a point. I guess at this point we should find out what we can about Park and Kim Lee, as well as Captain Jack."

"We could ask Park and Kim to lunch to get a feel for why they might be on the island, like we did with Charles and Piper," Zak suggested.

"Okay. Let's try to set it up for tomorrow. In the meantime, I'll see if I can get anything more out of Toad. If Park really is a suspect they must have a reason for adding him to the list. Maybe their reason has to do with information we don't yet have."

"I guess we should head back," Zak said. "Charlie looks like he's getting tuckered out."

I looked at my small dog, who did look like he was ready for a nap.

"Yeah. Let's. I want to talk to Ellie before we turn in. I know she planned to call Levi this evening. I suppose that by now he's made a definite decision about the job."

Zak went in to check his e-mails, while I stayed out on the patio to speak with Ellie, who was relaxing with a glass of wine.

"Did you get hold of Levi?" I asked after I poured a glass of wine for myself.

"Yeah. We talked for a long time, actually."

"And . . . ?" I prepared myself for the worst. I almost hated to even hear the answer.

Ellie looked directly at me. She smiled. "And I think he's going to pass on the job offer."

"Really?" I had to admit I was surprised by this. Everything I'd heard up to this point indicated that he wanted to take the job. "What happened?"

Ellie settled in for the explanation. "I told you that he stayed to work out with the team, which it turns out was a wonderful idea."

"Go on."

"One of the seniors on the team was on the Ashton Falls High School team four years ago. He told Levi that if it hadn't been for him, he would never have been able to attend college. I guess he got a free ride on a football scholarship and now has plans to attend medical school when he graduates next spring. According to Levi, the kid was flunking out of school until Levi got hold of him. Levi not only encouraged him to join the football team but made sure he attended his classes and turned in his work. He even lined him up with a tutor. The guy, who now plans to be a neurosurgeon, told Levi that he completely changed his life. He said his only plan when they first met was to drop out and try to get a job in a convenience store."

"Wow. That's really awesome. I bet that made Levi feel really good."

"It did. Levi also told me that the job at the college is very structured and won't provide him the opportunity to really work with the kids one on one. He would be the assistant to the assistant, and although there's room for advancement if he does well, he realized that he likes being a big fish in a small pond, where he can make the decisions and enter into personal relationships with the boys he coaches. He's going to talk to the head coach tomorrow, and then he plans to fly home on Sunday."

I hugged Ellie. "I'm so happy things worked out this way. For both of us, I don't know what I would have done if he'd moved away."

"Yeah. I've been pretty much a mess ever since I found out about the job. I love Levi so much, but this situation has given me some things to think about."

"Like what?" I asked.

"The fact that neither Levi nor I put the other one first in making the decision as to how to proceed makes me wonder if we're meant to be a couple."

"He's coming home," I pointed out.

"He is. But he's turning down the job because he realized he prefers the job he has. He didn't turn it down because of me. And when I thought he was going to take it, I realized I wasn't willing to move to be with him. I think that says something."

"You aren't going to break up with him?"

"No. But I'm going to take the time to really take a good hard look at our relationship. When I wanted children and he didn't, we let that make a difference.

It was only after the conflict was removed, when I found out I couldn't have children, that we allowed ourselves to move our relationship to the next level. And then he was offered this job, and once again neither of us was willing to sacrifice for the other. I really believe that if we were as committed as we should be, not being together wouldn't even be an option."

I hugged Ellie. I had to admit I didn't think she was wrong. In my heart, I knew I'd follow Zak anywhere.

Chapter 9

Saturday, August 1

"Good morning." I breezed into Toad's office armed with coffee and doughnuts.

"Are those for me?" Toad's eyes lit up.

"Yup. I figured you might enjoy a Saturday morning treat."

Toad accepted the offering but looked at me suspiciously. "What do you want?"

"What makes you think I want anything?"

He held up one of the doughnuts.

"What I want is to speak to Chandella without being tossed in jail," I admitted.

I explained that we'd learned that Jensen had only invited Ricardo to the dinner that night after Chandella requested that he do so.

"I would be interested in learning why Ricardo wanted to be on the boat in the first place," I added.

"Yes, that might prove to be useful information."

"Which is why I think one or both of us should speak to her."

"Chandella doesn't like me. I doubt she'll tell me anything. I guess it would be okay for you to speak to her, as long as you promise to come back to fill me in on the outcome of your discussion."

"Deal."

"And as long as you are coming back, bring me a couple more of these doughnuts. Chocolate. It's not often that I have a chance to sample any of the pastries they make for the resort."

"They don't sell these in town?"

"No. The pastry chef works for the resort." Toad finished off the first of the two I'd brought.

"The bakery at the resort is within walking distance," I pointed out. "If you like these doughnuts so much, you could just walk over and buy some."

"I'm not allowed on the resort."

"What do you mean, you aren't allowed on the resort? Whyever not?"

"No one from town is allowed on the resort except to work, and even then their movements are monitored."

I frowned. "What are you talking about?"

"Haven't you noticed the gate you must acess to come and go from the resort?"

"Yes, but I figured it was just to keep track of who came and went. You're telling me that no one from town is allowed on the resort grounds except if they work there?"

Toad bit into another doughnut. "I believe that is what I just said. Mr. Ewing doesn't want his rich guests mingling with the villagers. The only way a local can get onto the grounds of the resort is by a separate gate that is guarded at all times. When locals check in for their shift, they are provided with a tracking device that must be turned in at the end of each shift. If you work at the laundry, you had better go to the laundry and nowhere else or you will be fired immediately."

"That's insane."

Toad shrugged. "Have you enjoyed your vacation as much now that you have seen what the lives of the people who wait on you are really like?"

"No," I admitted. "In fact, I told the maid that she didn't need to clean up yesterday and I gave her a big tip as well."

Toad smiled a sort of lopsided smile. "Most of the guests of the resort never leave the grounds. They enjoy the benefits of first-class pampering without having to suffer a guilty conscious. Mr. Ewing works very hard to keep it that way."

"But you're law enforcement," I argued. "I don't see how Mr. Ewing can keep you out."

"The resort is private property. I assure you that no one, including me, is allowed onto the resort without either owner approval or a really good reason."

"I'm so sorry." I placed my hand on Toad's arm. "I'll bring you back a whole bag of doughnuts when I come back, and maybe while you're eating them you can fill me in on what you know about Park Lee and Captain Jack."

"Bring a dozen."

"A dozen it is."

"Do you know if Candy was working?" Toad asked.

"Candy?"

"Short. About your height. Blond hair that brushes her waist and the bluest eyes you've ever seen."

I pictured the short, chubby blond woman who had served me the doughnuts. She'd had a net over her hair, but I could tell it was long.

"Do you have a crush on her?" I knew I was correct in my assumption when Toad's chubby face turned bright red.

"If Candy is the woman with the—" I paused. What was the polite way to put it?

"Big nose," Toad said helpfully. "Yes, that's her."

"Then yes, she was working when I was there earlier. Do you want me to say hi for you?"

Toad shook his head frantically. "No, don't do that. Just find out if she is going to the movie tonight."

"I will."

I left Toad's office and headed back to the resort. I knew Chandella lived and supposedly worked at the resort, so I figured that was where I was most likely to find her. I couldn't get anyone to tell me where to find her and she wasn't in the executive offices, so it took longer than I anticipated to track her down. I eventually found her tanning near the pool; based on the dark tone of her skin, I assumed that was where she spent a lot of her time. It was obvious she devoted a lot of time to working on her body. She was gorgeous.

"Chandella?"

She opened one eye and looked at me. "Yes?"

"My name is Zoe. I was wondering if I could speak to you for a moment."

Chandella sat up. I turned away while she slipped a shirt over her bare breast.

"You are the woman Zak married."

"I am. Do you know Zak?"

Chandella smiled like the cat who stole the cream. "Yes. We are acquainted. What can I do for you?"

I really wanted to ask how exactly she knew Zak but decided that rational Zoe and not jealous Zoe would do best in this conversation.

"I wanted to ask you about Ricardo Jimenez. I understand you arranged for him to be invited on the dinner cruise the night he was murdered."

Chandella shrugged. "So?"

"I saw him grab you that morning and pull you into the breezeway. You didn't look happy to see him."

"I wasn't. The guy is a bottom feeder."

Chandella took a sip of her drink, which looked a lot like a mai tai despite the fact that it was at least two hours until lunch.

"If you didn't even like the guy why did you agree to talk to Jensen about inviting him on the cruise?"

"Why do you want to know?" she asked.

"At this point I'm afraid I'm still the prime suspect in his murder. I didn't do it, so I'm trying to figure out who did."

"I wasn't even on the boat," Chandella said.

I took a deep breath. "I realize that. I'm not accusing you of anything. I'm just trying to figure out why he was on the boat."

Chandella looked me up and down. I waited for her to decide whether to confide in me. I wouldn't be surprised if she decided not to. She didn't know me from Adam and had no reason to care about my possible incarceration.

"Ricardo knew I cheated on Jensen," Chandella eventually shared. "He threatened to tell him if I didn't get him an invite, so I did. I don't know why he wanted to be there. He didn't volunteer the information and I didn't ask. I don't know who killed him, but the guy was a lowlife I won't miss one tiny bit."

Chandella pulled her shirt over her head and tossed it aside. She laid back down on her stomach, as if to communicate that the discussion was over.

"What do you mean, you cheated on Jensen?" I asked. "He's married. He's cheating on Della with you. I'm not sure how you can cheat on him."

Chandella answered without so much as lifting her head. "Jensen has a wife and several mistresses. He provides for all of us, and in exchange we're all expected to be faithful to him. If he found out I was cheating he would cut me off financially and ban me from the resort."

"So you all know about one another?"

"We do. Can you spray some of that tanning lotion on my back?"

I did as she asked. If I had to guess, any of the men in the area would have been happy to comply if I hadn't been around.

"And you're happy with this arrangement?" I asked. I was finding this conversation difficult to stomach.

Chandella opened her eyes and lifted her head from the pillow she was resting on. "Sure. Why not? Jensen is a wealthy man. None of us want for anything. I really can't see giving up what I have to enter into a monogamous relationship with a man who would expect me to live in squalor. Now, if I could land a rich man like Zak that might be a different story."

"You stay away from Zak."

Chandella winked and laid her head back down. "We'll see."

I left Chandella and went back to the resort bakery to buy the dozen doughnuts I'd promised Toad, then headed back into town. Zak had texted to inform me that he'd arranged for us to have lunch with Park and Kim at one o'clock. That meant I wouldn't have a lot of time to drill Toad about the other two suspects, but hopefully, combined with what Zak was able to dig up, it would be enough to help me steer the conversation I hoped to have with the couple while we dined.

"A dozen chocolate doughnuts and a fresh cup of coffee." I set my offering on Toad's desk. "And yes, Candy is going to the movie tonight."

Toad smiled. "Did you track down Chandella?"

"I did. It seems Jimenez had some kind of proof that she'd cheated on Jensen and threatened to tell him about it if she didn't arrange the invite. Unfortunately, she didn't know why he wanted to be on the cruise. Personally, I think it might have had something to do with Park Lee."

Toad shoved half of a doughnut into his mouth. He chewed loudly and swallowed before he replied. "Why do you say that?"

I shared my suspicion that Park had been manipulating things the entire evening. He'd been the one to send me for the knife in the first place. He'd disappeared in order to go to the men's room after I left to fetch it and hadn't reappeared until after I found the body. It was his wife who'd discovered me in the hall with the body, and she was the one who had alerted the others.

"Admittedly, I can't prove anything, which is why I'd hoped you could share with me what you know about him," I concluded.

"And why would I do that?"

"Because deep in your gut you know I'm innocent?" I tried.

He rolled his eyes.

"Because I'll bring you another dozen doughnuts tomorrow morning?"

That earned me a smile. Toad shrugged. "Guess it couldn't hurt. You seem to have figured out pretty much everything we suspect anyway."

I sat down on the chair on the other side of his desk and waited for Toad to continue. If I knew the man could be bought for a box of doughnuts, I would have started bringing them days ago.

"Okay, what do you know that I haven't figured out?" I asked.

"Park Lee and Ricardo Jimenez visited the resort during the same span of days two months ago. During that time, they were seen together often. It is not the norm for vendors and guests to mingle; Jensen tries to keep the vendors and guests separate, as he does guests and employees."

"Go on," I encouraged when Toad stopped talking.

"You will bring coffee with the doughnuts tomorrow?"

"A whole thermos," I promised.

"While it is Jimenez's normal pattern to visit the resort every couple of months, it is not Park Lee's pattern to make a return visit so soon after he was here. What is even odder is that Jimenez and Park Lee arrived on the same day."

"When was that?" I asked.

"The Sunday before you arrived on Monday."

Interesting.

"Is that all?" I asked.

"For now. Bring me the doughnuts tomorrow and I will see if I can remember anything else."

I could see our conversation was over so I stood up. "We'll both be at the fund-raiser this evening, so can we count that as my evening check-in?"

Toad considered my request.

"I guess that would be acceptable. And remember, if you stumble over any new information, you are to find me immediately."

"I will. I promise."

By the time I got back to the house it was time to get ready for our lunch. Zak filled me in on his morning while I got changed.

"The deposits into the offshore account have all been made in the past four months. Each deposit was for twenty thousand dollars and there were five deposits in all."

"Wow; that's a lot of money. Who made the deposits?"

"Park Lee is the only name of the five I recognize. I checked the others against resort records and all five guests have stayed here during the past four months. Likewise, all five stayed in the VIP section. All five men rented sailboats, ate in the VIP dining room, took advantage of spa services, and went parasailing and scuba diving. It also appears that all five men participated in private card games hosted by Jensen. "

"Toad mentioned that Park and Kim were here two months ago and that the span of days they stayed mirrored the days Ricardo was here. He also told me that while it's Ricardo's normal pattern to visit the resort every couple of months, Park usually doesn't visit so frequently. Can you zip this up for me?"

I turned my back so Zak could zip the sundress I'd chosen to wear.

"That fits the timeline. We can verify all the dates Ricardo was here, but it appears the payments to his account began shortly after a visit four months ago."

"So how do you want to play this?" I asked Zak as I slid a pair of sandals onto my feet.

"We'll just engage in conversation like we did with Charles and Piper and then wait for an opening to do a little digging."

"How's my hair?"

"Your hair is great."

"Okay, then I guess I'm ready."

Zak had made reservations at the same restaurant where we'd had lunch with Charles and Piper. Zak suggested it because it was in the VIP section of the resort, and it seemed most VIPs didn't venture out to the main part of the resort. I quickly agreed because I was hoping to get another look at Jimbo. Despite the fact that Zak continued to insist that Jimbo had been working at the restaurant on the night of the murder, I wasn't convinced.

As we had when we lunched with Charles and Piper, we began the conversation by asking about neutral topics. Like Charles and Piper, Park and Kim traveled extensively and, as with the British couple, they had a lot of interesting stories to share. I tried to be patient, but I found it hard to concentrate on their trip to Greece when all I was really interested in hearing about was their trip to the island two months earlier.

"Jensen mentioned you're frequent visitors to the island," Zak finally commented after Park got up to go to the men's room. Waiting until Kim was alone was a good strategy; she seemed to be the chattier of the pair.

"Yes, we come every year or two," Kim answered.

"It's really a beautiful place," I added.

"We love it here," Kim confirmed. "In fact, this is our second trip this year."

"Wow, you really must love it here," I added.

"It really is quite a long journey. Park had some business he needed to check on or we probably wouldn't have come again so soon."

"Business?" I asked.

"I'll have to let him tell you about it when he returns. Oh, here he is now," Kim said as Park returned to the table.

"I was just telling Zak and Zoe that we were on the island to conduct some business," Kim said as soon as he sat down.

Park frowned. He didn't look overly upset that Kim had mentioned business, but he didn't seem thrilled either.

"Yes, well, I am involved in business ventures all over the world," Park answered vaguely.

"So is Zak," I added. "He has to travel quite extensively. I don't always go along, but if he decided to get involved in a business venture on the island I wouldn't mind a return trip. It's absolutely gorgeous."

"Maybe Zak can get in on Park's deal," Kim suggested. "It sounds really exciting."

Park shot her a stern look and she lowered her eyes.

"Ricardo Jimenez mentioned something to Zak about a business venture before he died, but he never did have the opportunity to get all the details," I fished.

Park looked at Zak. "I guess if Ricardo was considering cutting you in, he must have checked you out and been satisfied as to what he'd found."

"Cut me in?"

"On the treasure hunt," Park whispered.

"Treasure hunt?" Zak asked. "Ricardo didn't tell me what the business venture was; he just suggested that we needed to talk," Zak lied. In reality, Zak had never spoken to him at all.

"Ricardo and the others were being very selective about who they let in on the deal," Park confirmed. "I was lucky to have been in the right place at the right time. I really don't know what is going to happen now that Ricardo is dead."

"Would you mind filling me in?" Zak asked. "I never did get the opportunity to speak to him and I find you've piqued my interest."

Park paused, as if to consider Zak's request. He shrugged. "I guess it couldn't hurt. Maybe you can still speak to Jack about it."

"Captain Jack?" Zak verified.

"He is in charge of the operations end of the venture." Park looked around, as if to make sure no one was listening to what he was about to tell us. "When I visited two months ago I decided to cross something off my bucket list and learn to scuba dive. The instructor told me about a wreck he'd found that supposedly was worth tens of millions of dollars in today's market. He could see I was interested, so he volunteered to take me out to the site. We dove down as far as we could without specialized equipment, but the skeleton of the ship was clearly visible. I told him that I was interested in getting in on the action, so he hooked me up with Ricardo, who was taking care of the business end of things."

"Wow, how awesome would it be to dive on a sunken ship," I said enthusiastically. "Do you know which ship they found?"

"*The Carolina*. She was a British ship that sank in this area in 1764. Ricardo explained that although they'd located the ship, they couldn't bring up the treasure until they could raise enough money to invest in the equipment they would need. He seemed knowledgeable about both the history of the ship and the process that would be required to salvage it. He even had several items from the ship with the crest of the family that owned her on it. I checked out the history of the vessel, and when it lined up with what he'd told me, I agreed to help fund a portion of the project in exchange for a percentage of the salvage. Ricardo said they would begin salvaging the boat on August first, and he invited me to go along with the crew. I can't remember the last time I've been this excited about anything. Now, with Ricardo's death, I don't know what is going to happen."

Zak sat back in his chair. He appeared to be processing this information. Either that or he was planning his next question.

"It's a shame I missed the opportunity to get in on the deal." Zak sighed. "It sounds like a fascinating adventure. I'm sure the others will go ahead with the salvage. It sounds like Ricardo's job was simply to fundraise. If he has completed that task the men in charge of the actual operation should be able to go ahead as planned."

Park smiled. He seemed satisfied with Zak's explanation. "I hope so. I'd hate to miss out on being a part of history."

Chapter 10

The beach was packed with locals lounging on blankets, waiting for the movie to begin, by the time we arrived. One of the first things I noticed was the lack of resort guests in the mix. Thinking back, I hadn't seen an announcement about the event anywhere on the resort grounds. I supposed Jensen didn't want to encourage his guests to leave the grounds of the resort for any reason if he really was trying to create the illusion that the entire island was some sort of upper-class utopia.

"Maybe we should have mentioned this to a few of the others," I said to Zak. "I bet Dezi and Lucinda would have enjoyed spending time among the locals, and Charles and Piper seem to be the sort who are always up for an adventure."

"I don't know," Zak replied. "I think a lot of the resorts guests prefer to exist in a state of denial about the reality of living in such an isolated environment in which the division of the classes is extreme at best."

"Maybe, but if the group sponsoring the event really wants to raise enough money to build a shelter they're going to need to find a way to appeal to donors who have big bucks."

"I brought my checkbook." Zak smiled.

I smiled back. I sure loved this man.

"It looks like Sebastian is working the snack shack," Ellie commented after we'd spread our blanket on a grassy patch on the hill. "I think I'm going to go over to say hi. Maybe I'll offer to help."

"Have fun," I called as Ellie trotted away.

"Some of the kids from the club are sitting with Oria and a couple of the other counselors," Scooter pointed out. "Is it okay if I go say hi?"

"Sure," Zak answered. "But don't go anywhere else. I don't want to have to worry about losing you in the crowd."

"I'll go with him," Alex volunteered. "We'll be back before the movie starts."

"And then there were two." I grinned at Zak.

"Which sounds just about perfect."

I lay back onto the blanket with Charlie next to me and looked up at the stars, which were just beginning to make an appearance. It would be dark enough to begin the movie in another thirty minutes or so, but for now I was happy just enjoying the beautiful view provided by Mother Nature. The sound of the waves crashing onto shore in the background threatened to lull me into the state of unconsciousness commonly known as sleep.

"You still awake?" Zak asked.

"Um."

"It looks like Toad is headed this way. Weren't you supposed to check in with him when you got here?"

"Yeah." I yawned. "I was."

I sat up and waved to the short man, who was dressed casually in jeans and a T-shirt this evening.

"Evening, Toad," I greeted him as he approached the blanket.

"Evening." He nodded toward both Zak and me. "Can I talk to you?" He was looking directly at me. "Alone."

"Yeah, sure." I rolled over onto my knees and then stood up. "Can you keep an eye on Charlie?" I asked Zak.

"Charlie and I will keep the home fires burning while everyone else deserts us," Zak teased.

"Should we take a walk?" I turned my attention to Toad.

He nodded.

"I'm sorry I forgot to check in with you right away," I told him. "We really just arrived."

"It's fine. I really wanted to ask you about Candy."

"Candy?"

"How did she seem when you went back for the second batch of doughnuts today?"

"Seem?" I asked as we made our way down to the beach and away from the crowd.

"Did you tell her I said hi?"

"I did."

"And . . . ?" Toad asked.

I stopped walking and turned to look at him. "And she sort of blushed, lowered her eyes, and told me to tell you hi back."

Toad grinned.

"If you like her so much why don't you just go and talk to her? I saw her earlier, so I know she's here."

"Oh, no, I can't." Toad looked panicked.

"Why not?"

"I can't talk to girls."

"You're talking to me," I pointed out.

"What I mean is that I can't talk to girls I'm interested in dating. I get all tongue-tied and never know what to say."

I put my hand on Toad's shoulder in a demonstration of support. "Here's the way I see it: You can give in to your nervousness and never speak to the woman. I gather she's as shy as you are, so you'll most likely both live out your lives always wondering if the other was *the one*. Or you can strap on a pair and go say hi. Maybe she returns your affection and maybe she doesn't, but if you don't at least initiate contact you'll never know."

"Strap on a pair of what?" Toad asked.

"Never mind. My point is that you have a lot more to lose by not speaking to her."

"But what would I say?"

"Start with hi. If she says hi back maybe you ask her if she'd like to sit with you during the movie. If that goes well maybe at the end of the evening you ask her out."

"Ask her out?" Toad looked panicked again. "Like on a date?"

"Yes. A date. You know, maybe dinner and a movie. That type of thing."

"And then what?" Toad wondered.

"And then you start seeing each other on a regular basis, you fall in love, get married, and have a couple of kids with whom you can share this awesome island."

Toad smiled. "You really think all of that could happen?"

I hesitated. I really didn't know what was on Candy's mind, so I hated to overpromise. "I don't know if all of that will happen, but I do know that the only way it could happen is if you make the first move."

Toad hesitated.

"What's the worst that can happen?"

"She could laugh in my face."

"She might. But if she does, at least you'll know how she feels and you can stop wondering."

"Okay."

I looked back toward the crowd. "There she is. She's standing near the back and she's alone. Just walk over and say hi and then let fate take it from there."

Toad took a deep breath. "Okay. I'll do it."

I watched as he walked slowly toward the woman of his dreams. The odd-looking pair sort of reminded me of Shrek and Princess Fiona when she was in her ogre state. Neither were much to look at, but I had the sense that they could share a deep and meaningful love if they could just get past their shyness. Toad looked back at me just before he arrived at the spot where Candy was standing. I motioned him forward, holding my breath as he took his last awkward steps.

Please let her say yes.

I watched as he approached and said hi. Then I saw her smile shyly and say hi back. After a few exchanges of dialogue Candy led Toad to a blanket she had already set out.

Whatever else happened, Zoe Donovan had done her good deed of the day.

I was about to return to Zak and Charlie when I noticed a man who looked an awful lot like Jimbo skirting the crowd. I changed direction at the last minute and followed him. I know that according to everyone, the man I'd encountered on the yacht couldn't have been the man I was introduced to at the restaurant, but I happen to have very good eyesight and a very good memory and I know what I saw.

The man was moving quickly, purposefully, through the crowd. I tied to keep up with him without being too obvious, but I lost him once he hit the crowd that had gathered on the beach. I looked around, but there were too many people for me to find him, so I returned to Zak and Charlie.

"Everyone still gone?" I asked Zak when I reached the blanket where he was waiting with Charlie.

"Scooter came by to say he and Alex wanted to watch the movie with the other kids if that was okay. I told him it was. I haven't seen Ellie."

I sat down on the blanket. "I can go check on her if she doesn't show up in a few minutes." I looked around. "It's a lot more crowded than I thought it would be. I hope they make enough money to get the shelter off the ground."

"I'm sure they will," Zak assured me. "Did everything go okay with Toad?"

I filled Zak in on the Toad and Candy love story.

"It's usually not a good idea to get involved in other peoples' love lives," Zak warned me.

"I know." I shrugged. "I'm not involved. I just got them started." I looked around the crowd again. "I saw Jimbo earlier. I don't suppose he came this way?"

"Haven't seen him. You aren't still hung up on the fact that you saw him on the yacht the night of the dinner party?"

"I know what I saw."

Zak laced his fingers with mine. "I know you believe Jimbo was the man you saw on the yacht, but three different employees at the restaurant where he works confirmed he was there the entire evening. Maybe you just saw someone who looks like him."

I frowned. I supposed that was possible.

"Does Jimbo have a brother?" I asked.

"I don't know."

"I bet Sebastian does. I want to go check with Ellie anyway." I kissed Zak on the lips. "I'll be right back. I promise."

Zak sighed. I know he wishes I'd let this whole Jimbo thing go, but he did seem to be my best lead. If Jimbo didn't do it, I'm not sure who did. Park was my second strongest suspect. He didn't seem to have a motive, but he did have opportunity. He'd seemed genuine when we spoke to him at lunch, but if there's one thing I've learned of late it's that those who are likely to kill are also likely to be good liars.

And then there was Captain Jack. I hadn't had a chance to speak to him yet. Maybe he'd be here this evening and I could work my way into a conversation with him. I thought about the other guests on the yacht. Based on the angle of the knife in Jimenez's back, it appeared the killer was most likely tall. At least six feet. That eliminated all of the women, and darn, I just realized that also eliminated Park.

"How's it going?" I asked Ellie as I approached the snack booth. The snacks that were being offered included shrimp kabobs, steak and mushrooms on a stick, mini tri-tip sandwiches, and bite-size lobster rolls, among others. Ellie was wearing a white chef's toque and looked to be in her element.

"I'm having the best time." Ellie grinned. "Sebastian is a genius with simple yet elegant finger foods. Try these stuffed mushrooms. They have crab and lobster and are totally to die for."

I took one of the mushrooms. It was good.

"Sebastian brought an amazing display of desserts to donate to the cause as well. There's a separate booth set up over there." Ellie pointed to a small tent not far away.

"So you're planning to stay to help?" I asked.

Ellie shrugged. "Yeah. I thought I might. If Sebastian will have me."

Sebastian must have heard Ellie's reply because he turned from the customer he was waiting on and assured me that Ellie was more than welcome to stay.

"Okay, well, if you change your mind we have a blanket set up over near those rocks." I pointed into the distance.

"Try one of these shrimp kabobs before you go." Sebastian handed one to me.

"It's really good. What did you marinate the shrimp in?"

"A special homemade jerk."

"It really is wonderful." I grinned. "Can I take one for Zak?"

Sebastian handed me a second kabob. "Zak can have whatever he wants. According to Oria, his check will cover the cost of building the facility we need. It certainly was lucky the two of you decided to vacation here at this particular time."

"Yeah," I agreed. "Lucky."

I thought about Sebastian's statement. Was it lucky we decided to honeymoon here? It hadn't even been on our radar until Jensen Ewing presented the image of any idyllic family vacation to Zak. Could he have had a reason to bring us here? If so, I had no idea what that reason could be, but he had been fairly insistent that we take part in the dinner cruise. In fact, Zak had turned him down initially, but now that I thought back on it, Jensen had seemed prepared to counter every argument Zak had presented.

I decided to stop by the dessert tent to survey the offerings before heading back to Zak. I will say one thing for the residents of Heavenly Island: they certainly knew how to cook. All of the food I had tasted, without exception, had been absolutely fantastic.

The first thing I noticed when I walked into the tent was that Jimbo was manning it. I tried to appear casual as I headed to a display too fantastic to make choosing just one item possible.

"Wow. Everything looks so delicious."

"The desserts have all been donated by members of the shelter committee. They are all wonderful. Would you prefer cookies or cake?"

"Could I get a to-go box with a little bit of each?" I pulled a large bill out of my pocket and dropped it into the donation jar.

"Absolutely." Jimbo smiled.

"I tried to say hi when I saw you earlier down by the beach," I said casually as Jimbo filled my box.

"I've been here all night. You must have seen Malik."

"Malik?" I asked.

"My cousin. We look enough alike we could be twins. Even the locals get us confused at times." Jimbo handed me my box. "Thank you for your generous donation."

"I'm happy to help support the cause. I think a shelter is a wonderful idea. And the food you've all provided. Let's just say that it's the best I've had."

Jimbo smiled. "Thank you. We try."

"Is Malik a chef as well?" I asked, hoping Jimbo wouldn't find my question odd.

"No. Malik teaches scuba to the resort guests."

"I'd love to learn to dive," I commented, even though I was already a certified diver. Asking about a class would give me a good excuse to track the man down to speak to him. "Do you happen to have his contact information handy?"

Jimbo jotted a phone number down on a napkin. "You can usually reach him here. He has had some kind of project that he has been working on lately, so if he doesn't pick up go ahead and call him again. He is horrible about returning messages."

"Okay, thanks. I'll give him a call tomorrow."

I returned to Zak with the food, taking the long way around so I could pass close to where I'd last seen Toad and Candy to check on the couple. They were both seated on the blanket Candy had brought and seemed to be enjoying a humorous conversation, based on the smiles on both their faces.

Chalk one up for new love.

"What's all that?" Zak asked when I set the box of sweets down on the blanket. I have to confess I ate the shrimp kabob I'd meant to bring back for Zak as I was walking back from the dessert tent.

"A bunch of delicious-looking cakes and cookies. I spoke to Jimbo."

I explained about Malik and my plan to speak to him about scuba lessons.

"If you're going to take scuba lessons from this man I'm going with you," Zak insisted.

"I wasn't necessarily going to take lessons, I just figured calling about them would be a good excuse to talk to him."

"Either way, I'm going. If this man did kill Ricardo, I don't want you alone with him."

"Okay," I agreed. "I'll leave him a message that we're both interested in lessons. Maybe we can try to meet him tomorrow afternoon. I need to bring doughnuts to Toad, and I promised Alex I'd hike up to the old chapel with her in the morning."

"Sounds like a good plan. I told Scooter we could go surfing if the storm holds off for another day. Let's try to meet back at the house at around one."

Zak and I settled in as the movie started. I tried to focus on the story on the screen, but all I could think about were the clues rambling around in my brain. Park had said he'd found out about the salvage operation from the man who taught him to dive. Jimbo had just told me his cousin taught scuba to resort guests. The man I'd seen in the hallway had to have been Malik. The odds of there being three people on the island who looked like the man in the hallway was too huge even to consider.

I was trying to figure out what that might mean when I saw movement in the corner of my eye.

"I'm going to run to get another one of those shrimp kabobs," I whispered to Zak. "Do you want to try one?"

"Yeah, okay. Bring back a couple. Do you need some money?"

"I have some. I'll be back in a jiffy."

I got up and headed toward the edge of the crowd, where I had seen a man who I was pretty sure was Malik pass by. It took me a few minutes to pick up his trail, but eventually I saw him heading away from the beach, where almost everyone in town was gathered, and into the dense foliage of the interior. I knew it was going to be impossible to follow him through the darkness and was preparing to turn around to head back to Zak when I saw another figure step out from behind a clump of bushes. As I watched the pair greet each other, I suddenly realized there was another suspect to consider.

Chapter 11

Sunday, August 2

The next morning Alex and I headed up the narrow, rocky path that promised to take us from the beach to the top of the bluff where the chapel looked out over the sea. I had Charlie on a leash to ensure that he wouldn't take off chasing any of the wildlife that populated the island as we wound our way up the side of the cliff. There were a few clouds in the distance, but the sky overhead was clear. It seemed the rumors of a storm were wrong; it looked like it was going to be another glorious day.

"I think we may have underestimated the time it would take to get to the top," Alex commented when we were halfway up the steep, narrow path. "Maybe we shouldn't have told Zak we'd be home by one."

"The downhill trip will be quicker. I'm sure we'll be fine. If it starts to get to be too late we can call Zak to let him know we got hung up. It certainly is beautiful up here." I stopped to look out over the endless expanse of water. There were hundreds of seagulls circling overhead as they searched for their morning meal. The sea looked calm from our vantage point, but I knew that the section of shore we towered over was home to some of the largest waves on the island.

"What exactly did you learn about the church?" I asked as we both took a moment to enjoy the view.

"There were English settlers on the island in the eighteenth century. They didn't stay long—only a few decades, as far as the man who wrote the book could tell—but while they were here they built a few permanent structures, including the chapel."

"Why did they stay for such a short time?" I wondered as we continued up the trail.

"The English came to the island originally as survivors of a shipwreck. The natives who were here had boats, but nothing that would carry many people over a long distance, so the survivors settled in to wait for rescue. They lived here with the natives for fifty years or so until a hurricane wiped out all the island's inhabitants. There's a legend that a young couple hid in the church basement during the storm. They were the only survivors. When the hurricane was over they emerged and looked out over the calm sea. They thanked God for keeping them safe and promised to have many children to repopulate the island."

"I guess that's romantic in a depressing kind of way. What happened to the couple? Did they stay and repopulate the island?"

"The author of the book indicated that the tale of the two survivors was really more of a myth than the truth, but it's a nice story and it seems the population did grow, and the island was repopulated. Oh, wow."

We had just rounded a corner to reveal the fact that we'd made it to the top. It was breathtaking. Other than a graveyard and a small building that must be the chapel, the top of the bluff was totally clear. You could see for miles in every direction.

"Should we check out the chapel?" I asked. "It looks like the door is open."

"Yes, let's." Alex smiled.

"Hello," I called as we stepped inside the small structure. The building contained several rows of wooden pews, as well as a simple pulpit at the front of the room. There were no windows, but there was one overhead lamp that provided adequate light.

A robed man with a friendly face and a huge smile poked his head out from around a curtain that sectioned off one part of the building from the other. "Are you here for the service?"

"Service?" I asked.

"I hold a service here every Sunday," the man answered. "Oftentimes it is just me and Scout, but there are times when a few brave souls will make the hike to join me."

I looked at the small black dog that stood next to the man, who must have been in his sixties at least.

I looked at Alex. She nodded.

"Yes, I guess we are here for the service. Is it okay if Charlie stays?"

The man looked at Charlie. "Absolutely. Dogs bring the best energy. Scout and I discussed holding the service outside, if that is acceptable to you. It is such a beautiful morning."

"Outside would be great." I smiled. "You hold the service even when no one's here?"

"I do it for them." He nodded toward the well-kept cemetery. "All of these graves are over a hundred years old. Few bother to make the trip up the cliff to visit, so Scout and I make certain all the souls buried here have company at least once a week."

"That's really nice," Alex commented.

"If you will follow me this way, we will begin."

Alex and I followed the man back out into the sunshine.

"It really is a beautiful day," I commented.

"For now."

The short man seemed to have a well-rehearsed ritual, so Alex and I simply stood where he indicated we should and responded when asked to. We stood quietly and listened the rest of the time. Luckily, the service wasn't more than thirty minutes long, so we had time to ask a few questions before we needed to head back.

"I'd like to learn more about the history of the chapel," Alex said after the man indicated that the service was over. "It really is fascinating that it's the only structure on the island to have survived the big hurricane that wiped everything else out."

"The chapel was built on sacred ground. It is protected from the elements."

"Sacred ground?" I asked.

The man smiled at me but did not respond.

"Can you tell us anything else about the chapel?" Alex asked.

"I really must get back down the hill," the man responded. "You are welcome to have a look at the archives if you'd like. I'm sure you can find your answers there."

"Archives?" I inquired.

"They are in the basement. Come, I will show you."

The man showed us to an exterior door at the bottom of a set of steps situated below the foundation of the church. I opened the door and we stepped inside. It was cold and damp inside the underground room, which contained boxes filled with books and files. I looked around. There were a lot of boxes and all of them were covered with dust.

"There is a storm coming, so be sure to lock up when you leave."

I turned to ask the man for more specific instructions but he was gone. "That's odd. Did you see where he went?"

"No." Alex shook her head.

I shrugged.

"What do you think all this stuff is?" I asked as I picked up a dusty old book that was written in Spanish.

"I don't know. This stuff is really old. It looks like the documents date back to the time before the hurricane."

Alex picked up a book and opened the cover. She began thumbing through the yellow pages. "This book contains a history of all the ships that were lost in the area between fifteen hundred and eighteen fifty. I had no idea there were so many."

"I guess a lot of European settlers made the trip after the Americas were discovered, and I'm sure a good percentage of those were blown off course and ended up here. Are there any ships listed from 1764?" I asked.

"The boats are listed by half century rather than date, but there are several listed between 1750 and 1800."

I tried to remember the name of the ship Park hoped to salvage. "Does it list the names of the ships?" I asked.

"Yes, in most cases. Are you looking for something specific?"

"*The Carolina.*"

Alex flipped through a few pages. "Here it is." Alex began reading. "It was an English ship carrying a dowry. Why do you ask?"

"Someone told me the wreck had been found and that they planned to salvage it."

Alex smiled. "I guess it would be fun to read about it. Can we stay for a while to see what we can find?"

I hesitated. The trip down the narrow path would be a lot quicker than the one up, but the man we'd met, whose name we hadn't learned, had warned of the storm despite the abundant sunshine.

"For a little while, but we should keep an eye on the weather. It's sunny now, but I imagine these storms can blow in pretty fast."

Alex looked like a kid in a candy shop as she settled in with a stack of dusty old books. I wondered if Zak and I were doing the right thing to even consider moving her to Ashton Falls to be educated by a group of senior citizens. Granted, the seniors in question were all very intelligent and well-educated, and Alex really was exceptional. But she was only ten, and a stable home life was probably as important as anything for her healthy development into adulthood.

Alex was completely entranced, so I picked up a book and began to read about the various ships that had been reported lost in the area. Based on the number of ships that fell to either pirates or storms, I don't think I would have wanted to set out across the ocean during that particular period in history. On the other hand, I supposed every period in time had its own inherent dangers.

"What was that?" Alex said quite a bit later. I'd become engrossed in the story of a ship that sank in the area hundreds of years ago and had completely lost track of time.

"I don't know." I set the book down. "It sounded like something hitting the side of the building. Stay here while I check it out."

I opened the door and was greeted by a wall of wind and rain. The storm had arrived and we hadn't even been aware of it.

"That was the wind blowing something against the side of the building. I'm afraid the storm snuck up on us. We'd better wait here until it passes," I explained.

Alex looked concerned. "Do you think we'll be okay?"

I made sure the door was shut tight, then sat down next to Alex. She was shaking like a leaf. She seemed to take most things in stride so I was surprised by her fear.

"Of course we'll be fine." I pulled her into my arms. "Didn't you say this building survived that big hurricane?"

"Yeah. I did say that."

"And this is just a little rain by comparison. Besides, the room we're in is below ground level, making it extrasafe, and the man we met assured us the church is built on sacred ground and therefore protected."

There was another loud bang as the wind blew another large object into the wall of the church facing the ocean. I had to admit it sounded like the building was going to come down on top of us.

Alex scooted closer as the wind whistled through a small crack in the wood surrounding the doorway.

"I should call Zak to let him know we're okay," I suggested. "He's probably worried that the storm hit while we were hiking back."

"Okay." Alex scooted away slightly to give me room to dial.

The phone was dead. "I guess the storm has knocked out the signal."

Alex began to shiver, even though it was balmy and not at all cold.

"Did you find more information about *The Carolina*?" I asked in an attempt to divert her attention from the sounds outside.

"Some." Alex looked around nervously.

"It would be fun to find a treasure like that," I commented.

Alex jumped. "Did you hear that? It sounded like the roof came off."

"I don't think it was the roof."

Alex looked white.

"I bet the locals who found *The Carolina* are excited to see what they can pull off her," I said, once again trying to distract her from the storm.

Alex let out the breath she had been holding and looked at me. "I don't think they'll find anything. *The Carolina* was found and salvaged over a hundred years ago. I'm afraid the men who think they found the treasure will be disappointed."

"Yes, I guess they will. That's really too bad. It seems like they went to a lot of trouble to attract investors to pay for the salvage operation."

"It seems like they should have researched the history before they began," Alex reasoned. "The information was right there in the book. I'm sure it can be found in other archives as well."

"It does seem they should have researched the matter."

Alex screamed as the entire building shook. The wind really was getting bad. I put my arm around Alex and pulled her close. "It's okay," I assured her.

I stroked her hair as she trembled in my arms.

"Have you always been afraid of storms?" I asked.

"Not always. When I was in the first grade there was a bad storm that destroyed part of the boarding school I was going to at the time. It was Christmas and most of the other girls were gone for the holiday. Part of the roof blew in and trapped me. I called for help, but no one came for hours. I was scared and alone. I've hated storms ever since."

"Oh, honey." I hugged her even tighter. "I'm so sorry. That never should have happened to you."

Alex didn't say anything, but I could feel her terror.

"How would you like to come to live with Zak and me this school year?"

I realized I might be premature in asking, but I hoped the conversation would distract her.

Alex pulled away slightly. She looked me in the eye. "Really?"

"We'll need to get your parents' permission first, but yeah, if they agree. Zak is going to arrange for you to attend the middle school in Ashton Falls for part of the day and then Phyllis and some of the others have agreed to homeschool you in the afternoons to fill in the gaps."

Alex's grin was wider than I had ever seen it. God, I hoped her parents would go for it. If not, she was going to be heartbroken.

"You aren't making this up just to distract me from the storm, are you?"

"I brought it up right now in an effort to distract you," I admitted, "but Zak and I have been discussing it, and the others have agreed to help out."

Alex let out a screech that sounded like a yelp as she wrapped her arms around my neck and held on tight. "There's nothing in this world I'd like more than to come to live with you and Zak. We could be a real family."

Chapter 12

We heard a helicopter land outside the building the minute the storm let up enough for it to set down. Apparently, my knight in shining armor had once again come to save me. The poor guy. He was frantic, thinking Alex and I had been caught on the narrow trail that wound its way along the cliff when the storm hit. I could tell by his look of relief that he was happy to see we were safe and dry inside the basement of the sturdiest building on the island.

The wind had all but stopped, but the weather forecast promised plenty of the wet stuff for another twenty-four hours at least. I'd never gotten around to calling Malik about the scuba lesson, but I imagined it was a moot point at this juncture anyway. I'd been thinking about everything I'd learned and I was pretty sure I'd figured things out. Now all I had to do was convince Talin I was right. Luckily, he answered when I called the number he'd given me and agreed to meet me at the jail.

"Okay," Talin began once we were seated in the same room in which he'd interrogated me. "What do you have?"

"As much as I hate to admit this, I believe Ricardo Jimenez, the dog-hating lowlife, was actually on the yacht to warn Park Lee that he was being scammed."

Talin looked surprised but not shocked by my statement. "Really? Can you prove that?"

"No," I admitted. "Not at this point."

"Perhaps you should start at the beginning," Talin suggested.

This time I'd made a point to use the ladies' room prior to my trip to the jail, so I was more than willing to take the long way around.

"After my lovely time in your jail I decided I most definitely didn't want to spend any more time here. And after getting to know Toad a bit, I realized that while he's a perfectly lovely man, he was never going to be able to solve Ricardo Jimenez's murder on his own. You seemed to have disappeared, and although you told me not to, I'm afraid I may have poked around just a tiny bit."

Talin didn't look surprised. "I expected as much."

"You did?"

"Your Sheriff Salinger told me that you would. He also assured me that you are very good at poking around. I've been watching you, but I decided to give you some rein to see where you took me. So what did you find?"

I don't know why I was surprised that Talin had been playing me the whole time, but I was. I was half-tempted not to share what I knew, but that would be childish, not to mention downright stupid.

"Zak found out that Jimenez had set up an offshore account to deal with the funding for a salvage operation he believed he was a partner in. There were five deposits into the account for twenty thousand dollars each. All five of the deposits were made by VIP guests of the resort. The only one of the men currently visiting the island is Park, so he's the only investor I've spoken to. I think we can assume all five men were exposed to a similar experience."

I paused.

"Go ahead," Talin encouraged.

"When I spoke to Park, he indicated that the man he took diving lessons from mentioned to him that he had found a sunken ship whose cargo appeared to be worth hundreds of millions of dollars. This of course piqued Park's interest, so he asked for more information about the wreck. The scuba instructor took him out to the dive site and had him dive down to the point where he could see the skeleton of the ship. He then showed Park some artifacts he'd brought up, as well as the ship's manifest, detailing the gold and jewels the vessel was carrying when it sank. Park, being the rich yet bored businessman he is, told the man he wanted in on the treasure hunt, so the instructor set him up with Ricardo, who had been put in charge of fund-raising for the operation."

"And who is this scuba instructor?"

"I believe his name is Malik. He's Jimbo's cousin and he looks exactly like the man I saw on the yacht the night Ricardo was murdered."

"So Malik and Ricardo were business partners?" Talin asked.

"That's the way it would appear, but I believe there's more to it than that."

"Why do you think so?" Talin asked.

"Last night I saw Malik at the movie. I followed him into the jungle, where he met a woman who was obviously his lover. It was Della."

Talin's eyes got big. "Della is cheating on Jensen with Malik?"

"Based on what I witnessed I'd say so. It also appeared, based on what I managed to see and overhear, they're very much in love."

"While that's a big piece of news, I don't see what it has to do with either the salvage operation or Ricardo's death," Talin pointed out.

"Bear with me, I'm getting to that. I found some of the facts I'd uncovered puzzling at best. For one thing, why did Malik cut Ricardo in on the deal in the first place? From what I've discovered, it appears Malik was the one who stumbled across the wreck. Yes, he'd need equipment to salvage the vessel, and that would take capital, but if it really was worth hundreds of millions of dollars, I would think he would have rich individuals seeking the thrill of an adventure lining up to invest in the project. Malik was the one with access to the rich guests. He was the one who sold Park and most likely the others on the idea of investing in the venture. Why cut in some random vendor?"

"Good question." I could see Talin was on the edge of his seat.

"At first I thought Ricardo might be blackmailing Malik. He seemed to be the observant type. He knew Chandella was cheating on Jensen, so maybe he knew Della was cheating on Jensen with Malik as well. I figured Ricardo heard about the treasure and wanted in, so he threatened to tell Jensen about Malik and Della if they didn't make him a partner."

I waited for Talin to catch up with the thought chain. It had taken me a minute to get there as well.

"But Jensen didn't even know Ricardo. That was what he said when I spoke to him after the murder. Why would he believe him over Della?"

I smiled but remained silent.

"Unless he had proof," Talin realized.

"Almost there," I encouraged.

"The baby. Della is carrying Malik's baby, and somehow Ricardo found that out. Malik is black; Della is white and so is Jensen. When the baby is born it will be obvious it isn't Jensen's. He will divorce Della and banish her from the island."

"Exactly."

"This is a good story, but do you have proof of it?"

"No," I admitted. "At this point it's just a theory."

"Okay, so Ricardo finds out about the baby and blackmails Malik into cutting him in on the treasure hunt. That still doesn't explain why Ricardo wanted to be on board the yacht the night of the dinner, or why Malik killed him that night. If Malik was tired of the blackmail why not kill him at a more convenient time?"

"I asked myself that same question, and the only answer I could come up with was that the blackmail wasn't the reason Malik killed Ricardo. In fact, I pretty much discarded the blackmail theory once I really thought it through, but I figured it was an important enough piece of the overall picture to bring it up."

Talin looked confused. "But I thought you just said you believed the reason Malik cut Ricardo in on the deal was because he was blackmailing him."

"That's what I thought for a while. I've since changed my mind."

"You are a complex woman, Zoe Donovan."

"So I've been told. I really am getting to the point, so just bear with me." I began to set the scene. "Malik and Della are in love. Della finds out that she's pregnant and realizes it's only a matter of time until Jensen finds out the baby isn't his. She feels entitled to a payout for her time in his service, so she and Malik come up with a plan to scam some of the VIP guests out of their hard-earned money. Malik knows about the wreck, and maybe he even has some artifacts he's collected over time. He comes up with the idea of selling shares in a salvage operation. Once the money is deposited into his account, he and Della can use it to start over again somewhere else. He realizes he needs a front man. A fall guy. So he decides to cut Ricardo into the deal."

"If Malik found a shipwreck worth hundreds of millions of dollars why would he settle for one hundred thousand dollars?" Talin asked. "Unless," he realized, "the ship is not really *The Carolina* and there is no treasure."

"No, I believe the ship is *The Carolina*, and there was a treasure at one point. When I was trapped in the church basement this morning I came across a book that listed all the shipwrecks in this area for the past three hundred years, as well as an accounting of the treasure on board and the current status of that treasure. *The Carolina* was an English ship that sank with a rich dowry in 1764. In today's market the value of the cargo would be worth hundreds of millions, if not billions of dollars. The problem was that the ship was harvested over a hundred years ago."

"So Malik is selling shares in a salvage operation related to a ship that has already been salvaged."

"Yes, I believe so." I took a breath before I continued. "And I believe Ricardo really did believe there was a treasure. I don't think it was until he returned to the island a few days ago that he realized he'd been duped. It seems the money that had been deposited into the account he'd set up to pay for the salvage operation had been transferred out of his account the day before the cruise. It was only after he was made aware of the transfer that he figured out that not only had he been had but he'd been set up to be the fall guy."

"Wouldn't it be too late to warn Park?" Talin asked.

"Zak found out that there's a forty-eight hour window in which the money is held after the transfer is initiated. I imagine Ricardo's urgency in gaining access to Park was to warn him before that time period was up."

"So if Mr. Jimenez did not set up the transfer from his account, why couldn't he stop it?"

"Zak looked into that. The account was set up by Ricardo and his name was on it, but Malik was the one who set up the password and thus had control over the money. I'm not sure why Ricardo couldn't stop the transfer after it was initiated, but I think we need to assume that wasn't an option. I believe Ricardo wanted an invite to the dinner party to gain access to either Park or Jensen or both. We know he blackmailed Chandella into getting him an invite at the last minute. I believe Malik found out Ricardo had obtained the invitation, so he snuck aboard and killed him. Of course, like I said, I can't prove it. We'll have to get him to confess."

"And how are we going to do that? We don't have any proof."

"I have a plan."

"I'm not surprised." I actually saw a look of admiration in Talin's eyes. "So what is your plan?"

"The transfer of the money was completed, so we should assume Malik is now in control of it. He and Della met last night in a semipublic place, so I have to assume they're ready to flee the island and may not care if Jensen finds out about the affair at this point. If they haven't already gone, which is doubtful due to the storm, we should assume they will once the weather clears up."

"We are expected to have steady rain for another twenty-four hours at least," Talin confirmed.

"Okay, so whatever we're going to do, we need to do it today."

"We?"

"Assuming you need my help of course. Which I'm willing to give, as long as I'm allowed to leave the island on Wednesday as planned."

I listened to the sound of the rain pounding on the metal roof of the old building while Talin contemplated the situation. I had to wonder if Jensen suspected Della had been cheating on him. Chances were he was too arrogant to even consider such a thing. I know I should be angry with Della and Malik for killing Ricardo and messing up my honeymoon, yet I couldn't help but remember the depth of the passion they seemed to share.

Still, they could have just left the island and earned their bread and butter by working hard and living frugally. Stealing from the rich guests at the resort might in some twisted way seem justified to them, but it was still stealing.

"All right. I agree to accept your help and I agree to let you leave on Wednesday as you have planned to do. So what is your plan?"

"We steal their money."

"Steal their money? How would we do that? It isn't even on the island."

"No, but it's sitting in an account Zak has already traced. We don't need to actually steal the money; we just need to set up false data so they think it's been transferred."

"Your Zak can do that?"

I shrugged. "Zak is a genius. I'm sure he can handle something like this, but he'll need access to better computer equipment than we brought with us."

"Mr. Ewing has the best computer equipment money can buy," Talin stated.

"I guess he needs to find out what's going on at some point."

It turned out that Jensen did have state-of-the-art technology at his disposal. It was really quite impressive. Zak knew his way around it because he had helped to set up the software, so putting our plan into play was a lot easier than I thought it would be.

I have to admit I felt bad for Jensen. I didn't think I would. On one hand, he'd been keeping multiple women and should have realized they might not all stay faithful to him, but he was devastated to hear our theory that the baby was most likely not his. Of course we still didn't know that for certain, but after we shared what we knew to be true, he admitted he'd been harboring a small amount of doubt.

Zak didn't need to actually steal the money. He simply planted information in Malik's account that made it look like the money had been moved. He followed that up with a text to Della, informing her of the transfer.

Jensen intentionally left Della alone in the house, so she was free to move about and do whatever it was she was going to do. Zak cloned her phone and replaced it with one we could listen in on.

The stage was set; now all we had to do was wait. Waiting, I'd learned from past experience, was often the hardest thing to do. I chatted with Talin about other cases he had worked on, while Zak spoke with Jensen about anything and everything to take his mind off his broken heart. It really was an odd gathering of individuals who sat around the listening device Zak had set up, waiting for something to happen.

"She's on the move," Zak eventually informed us. He was tracking her phone with the GPS that was installed.

We watched as Della left the resort and headed east. As expected, she ended up at the marina on the far end of the island. Talin had informed us that Malik lived on a boat at the marina. If the weather had cooperated they could very well have been long gone by the time we figured everything out.

"What did you do with the money?" we heard Della say, followed by the sound of a palm meeting flesh.

"I didn't do anything with it," Malik answered. "Why did you slap me?"

We assumed the silence was the result of Della showing Malik the text she had received about the transfer.

"What the hell?" Malik yelled. "Who could have done this?"

"You're the only person who comes to mind," Della insisted.

"Why would I transfer money out of an account we already control?" Malik reasoned.

"I don't know. Why would you?" Della confronted him. "Were you planning to take off without me?"

"Why would I do that? I love you."

"You were never happy about the baby. Maybe you decided to start over fresh with someone else."

"I wouldn't do that. I love you. You know I do."

There was silence, but it sounded like they were kissing.

"What are we going to do?" Della eventually asked.

Silence again.

"I don't know," Malik answered after a good long while.

"We could just wait until after the baby is born. It will give us time to come up with a new way to get some money," Della suggested.

"We can't wait. I killed a man. Eventually someone is going to put everything together. We need to figure out who stole our money and steal it back."

"How are we going to do that, Malik? Ricardo Jimenez is dead and Jack was the only other person who knew about this kind of thing. What do we know about tracing money transfers? You never should have killed him."

"Malik killed Jack?" I said aloud.

"That's the way it sounds," Talin answered. "When was the last time you saw him?" he asked Jensen.

"The night of the cruise."

We all quieted down to listen.

"He knew I killed Ricardo and he threatened to come clean," Malik stated. "He said he was on board with the swindle but he drew the line at murder. What was I supposed to do?"

"Maybe he was just using the fact that he knew you killed Jimenez to get a bigger cut of the pot. Did you ever think about that? If he was going to rat you out, why didn't he do it when he was questioned in the first place?"

I heard a loud crash. I don't know if something fell or Malik hit something like a wall.

"Damn," Malik yelled.

"Stop it; you're scaring me," Della cried.

Talin picked up a two-way radio. "We have enough. Go in and get him."

I knew that Toad and two other locals who had been deputized to help out when needed were waiting for Talin's signal to arrest the pair.

"Look at that." I turned to Zak. "I helped to catch the bad guy and I didn't even have to put myself in any danger."

Zak kissed me. "I hope this is the start of a trend."

I kissed Zak back. "I guess we'll see."

Chapter 13

Wednesday, August 5

On one hand, when Wednesday rolled around I was thrilled to be able to step onto Coop's private jet free of any restraints. On the other, I found I was really going to miss some of the people I'd met on our honeymoon. I knew in my gut that I wouldn't be back to the island. It turned out that ten days in paradise was more than I could take.

It looked like Toad and Candy had turned a corner. I might be premature, but I saw plump babies in their future. Talin and Jensen seemed to have come to some sort of an understanding, and I predicted a more relaxed relationship between Jensen and the locals. Jensen had even worked things out so that Della was put under some sort of house arrest until after the baby was born.

"So, was it everything you imagined a honeymoon would be?" Zak teased after we were underway.

"Totally." I grinned as an exhausted Charlie snored in my lap.

Ellie was taking a nap and Alex and Scooter were watching a movie.

"It's going to be hard to come up with something equally awesome for our one-year anniversary."

I put my head on Zak's shoulder. Once we'd gotten the case wound up on Sunday we'd spent Monday and Tuesday making up for lost time. Not only did we rent some horses for a once-in-a-lifetime ride on the beach but we surfed, hiked, swam, and made love on the beach. Ellie and the kids had tagged along for everything but that last part.

"Can you believe summer is almost over?" I asked. "Between wedding planning, wedding guests, honeymoons from hell, and planning the Academy, summer has slipped through our fingers. Still, I'm excited about our plans."

"I spoke to Alex's parents, and they're fine with our plan to have her come live with us," Zak informed me.

I smiled. "I'm glad. She was really excited about the idea. Is she still going to go for a visit with her parents?"

"Yeah. I've arranged for Coop to take her to the dig they're working in South America next week. He'll pick her up just before Labor Day and bring her back to Ashton Falls. I called the school she'd been attending and they're going to transfer all her records."

"And Scooter?" I asked.

"We're going to drop him at his grandparents on the way home and then I'll go pick him up at the end of the month. His grandparents have likewise agreed that it would be wonderful if he can live with us for the school year. I'm going to enroll him in Ashton Falls Elementary School. Now that he's calmed down a bit, I think he'll do best in that environment, and he's excited about going to school with Tucker and some of the other kids he left behind when he moved from Ashton Falls."

Zak turned and looked at me. "Mrs. Donovan-Zimmerman, it looks like you're about to become a surrogate mother."

I placed my hand on Zak's cheek. "As long as you're the surrogate father, I'm all in."

"That's good, because I finally got Pi to agree to our plan. It looks like we're going to be a family of five this fall."

I glanced toward the front of the plane, where Alex and Scooter were laughing at the movie. I will admit to having a few doubts about my ability to play surrogate mom to three children, especially when one of them was a streetwise teen who most likely outweighed me. But I loved Zak. And I loved Alex and Scooter. And I knew I would crawl to the ends of the earth for any of them.

"So if I'm hearing you right, we'll have the next three weeks or so all to ourselves?"

"We will. Why? Do you want to go somewhere?"

"Actually," I leaned close and whispered in Zak's ear, "I thought we might go home, stock the pantry with three weeks' worth of groceries, lock the door, and hang out a do-not-disturb sign."

"I like the way you think, Mrs. Zimmerman."

And They Lived Happily Ever After

Dear Reader:

Once I completed *Heavenly Honeymoon* I spent some time debating what to do next. The will-they, won't-they question in the Zoe and Zak story has in many ways come to completion. Yes, they may still have challenges to face as they build a family and live out their lives, but I think I can say with confidence that insecure Jealous Zoe is gone forever. I believe in strong relationships and happily ever after, and that's what I want for my favorite couple. Zak has more than proven his devotion to Zoe, and I think that after the many starts and stops, Zoe is finally fully confident in this love. I feel certain that from this point forward we'll see a more mature and confident protagonist.

Which, I realized, presents a quandary. In many ways I feel that the hook in the Zoe Donovan story has been a combination of the yin and yang in Zak and Zoe's relationship, as well as the quirky nature of Zoe's actions, which have been based, in part, on her lack of emotional maturity. If we have a newly mature protagonist in a strong and committed relationship, how can the overall story continue to evolve?

I contemplated several options. Should I end the series? Have Zak and Zoe's marriage turn out to be illegal after Zak finds out he was already married in a tribal ceremony in Tibet? Have Zoe get amnesia? After quite a bit of contemplation, I finally decided to go in another direction and step outside the box.

Beginning with the next book, *Hopscotch Homicide*, which will publish in August, there will be two or three chapters at the end of each Zoe Donovan mystery from a novel within a novel I am calling *The Zimmerman Academy*. This novel within a novel will be presented from the viewpoint of Phyllis King, a retired English professor.

If you've read *Soul Surrender* and *Heavenly Honeymoon*, you know Phyllis has been set up to take on a much more enhanced role than she has to this point. Personally, I think it will be fun to go along with this sixty-two-year-old woman as she experiences first love, raising teens, and finally breaking free of the cocoon in which she has wrapped herself for most of her life.

If you remember, Phyllis is a lifetime academic who turned her back on romance and family so she could focus fully on her academic career. We've seen, during the series, a hint of regret. The way she's taken on the role of grandma to Jeremy's daughter Morgan, as well as the way she seems to have taken Alex under her wing. She's already committed to Zak that she'll help with the Zimmerman Academy, and in *Heavenly Honeymoon*, it was revealed that she was willing to have a handful of teenage girls move in with her. If you ask me, Phyllis may be late to the gate, but it appears she's about to toss off the sequestered life she had chosen and start living.

I'm planning to make the new books somewhat longer than the Zoe books have been in the past. Be assured that Zoe is still the star, and we'll still be invited along on Zoe's personal journey as she settles into marriage, family life, and, eventually, pregnancy. Yes, she'll face personal challenges as she learns to be a mother to the stray children it appears she and Zak seem destined to collect, and, yes, Zak, Levi, and Ellie will be there to see her through it. However, we will see a new maturity in Zoe. She'll be more confident and quite a bit less needy than the Zoe we've seen to this point.

I struggled with whether to insert the chapters that are written from Phyllis's point of view into the Zoe Donovan mysteries chronologically, or to simply include them in the end as a separate short story.

I realized I would have fans who would prefer each of these approaches. Some of you won't want the Zoe narration interrupted by Phyllis's thoughts, and others will appreciate knowing what's going on behind the scenes in Phyllis's world in a chronological manner.

What I've decided to do is to include the chapters by Phyllis in the end but to insert hyperlinks that will take you to the side story and then return you to the point at which you veered away when you're done with that chapter. Readers who prefer this approach can flip back and forth between the two points of view and experience the story in true chronological fashion.

If you prefer to read the extra chapters as a separate short story, simply ignore the hyperlinks and continue on with the Zoe story.

Finally, for any of you who aren't interested in Phyllis's life at the Academy, you can simply skip those chapters. There won't be any clues pertaining to the murder in these chapters that aren't provided elsewhere. I hope this approach works for everyone.

I've included a sample chapter from the Zimmerman Academy at the end of this book. This is the actual first chapter in the story entitled *Zimmerman Academy* and will be included in *Hopscotch Homicide*, along with chapters 2 and 3. Chapters 4–6 will be included at the back of *Ghostly Graveyard*, and so on. I really think the new approach is going to be awesome and hopefully you will agree.

The Zimmerman Academy

From the Diary of Phyllis King

Chapter 1

Friday, September 4
Welcoming the Girls

Looking back, I knew in my gut that my life was about to change forever. As an intentionally isolated individual who had spent the past sixty-two years avoiding the complicated emotional entanglements that seem to come standard with interpersonal relationships, I found that I was a lot more nervous than I wanted to admit. I guess the first time I really let the effect of my actions sink in was the day the girls arrived. As I stood stoically in my living room, waiting for Armageddon to rain down, I felt the life I had built to that point slowly slipping away.

"Oh, lord, what have I done?" I asked my cat, Charlotte.

Charlotte wound her body around my legs in a circle eight pattern as I looked out the window. What made me think I could take responsibility for three teenage girls? Was I crazy?

Apparently.

When Zak talked to me about helping him with the Zimmerman Academy, I'm afraid I let sixty-two years of loneliness burst forth in an orgasmic eruption of helpfulness.

"Sure, I'd love to help you oversee development," I said aloud. "You want me to be the principal? It would be a dream come true. Help out with the teaching during this first year of transition? Absolutely." I looked down at Charlotte. "Whatever was I thinking?"

Charlotte stopped her journey through my legs and jumped up onto the table next to where I was standing. She knew she was not allowed on the table, but she also knew I was so far into my tirade that I wouldn't pay her the least bit of attention.

"I know I didn't have to offer to lodge the girls," I admitted. "It just seemed to make sense at the time. We do have a lot of extra bedrooms in this big, empty house."

Charlotte greeted my rant with a yawn, followed by a look of derision.

"Fat lot of help you are." I sighed. "Do you think it's too late to back out?"

Charlotte rolled her eyes. Or at least I imagined she'd roll her eyes if cats could actually perform such a task.

I looked out the window to the yard I'd so painstakingly nurtured. It was a lot of work, but my flower garden gave me such a deep feeling of serenity and contentment. I'd always wanted a cottage-style house despite the fact that I'd settled in the mountains. When I'd first seen the large two-story structure, which was so different from the log houses that populated the area, I knew I'd found the home I'd always dreamed of. The garden hadn't grown up overnight. It had taken years of love and nurturing to coax the seedlings into large and healthy plants. Over the years I'd found that gardening in an alpine environment can be challenging at the least.

I turned away from the window and looked around the room. I decided the baby grand piano really could use a good dusting even though I'd dusted that morning. I thought about heading toward the cleaning supply closet to look for a dust cloth, but I realized the girls wouldn't care about imaginary dust. I glanced at the clock. It was seven minutes after four. Hadn't Zak said they'd be here at four?

Charlotte jumped from the table to the windowsill and meowed. I looked out the spotlessly clean window just in time to see the large white van as it rolled to the curb.

Just breathe.

I took one last look at the surgically clean room and turned toward Charlotte. "They're here. Are you ready?"

Charlotte took one look at the crew that was piling out of the van, jumped off the windowsill, and took off up the stairs.

Traitor.

I took a deep breath and looked down at the pencil skirt I'd worn with sensible shoes and a white silk blouse. If there was ever an outfit that was all wrong for meeting a group of teenage girls for the first time this was it.

God, Phyllis, you are such an old maid. They're going to hate you.

As Zak helped the girls unload their things, I looked in the hallway mirror and considered the woman I'd become. Where had the years gone? It seemed like only yesterday that Bobby Davenport had asked me out on the one and only date I'd ever been asked on. I'd had a crush on the guy for over a year and couldn't believe he had actually noticed me. I remember that it felt like I was swimming in a pool of desire and excitement when he smiled at me. Which is why I'd, quite illogically, turned him down.

I'd used the pretext of having a history exam to study for, but I knew in my heart that wasn't true. At the time I don't remember making a conscious decision *never* to date, fall in love, or marry. In that moment all I'd *really* decided was that I was too scared to go on *that* date. I remember wondering how I'd gotten to be an elderly twenty-one years old without ever having been kissed. Everyone else I knew was well versed in the art of lovemaking by the time they'd reached their third decade, but me? I'd buried my face in a book, ignored the world, and missed my one and only chance at normal.

I touched my hand to the slight wrinkling around my eyes. I hadn't even noticed that my skin had begun to sag. It felt as if it had happened in a heartbeat. One moment I was a young and vibrant academic with a bright future ahead of her and the next I was an old woman living with a cantankerous cat.

"It's never too late for a new beginning," I coached myself as I tucked a lock of gray hair into a serviceable bun. "No need to fret about what could, would, and should have been. Today I will turn the page and begin a new chapter."

I ran a hand over the surface of the spotless coffee table one last time before I headed to the front door and opened it wide.

"Zak, Zoe." I held out my arms to the couple I'd grown to care for deeply. "I'm so happy you finally made it."

"Sorry we're late," Zoe said as she hugged me as soon as she arrived at the front door. "The traffic was a bear."

"I can imagine it would be, given the holiday."

"Phyllis King, this is Eve, Pepper, and Brooklyn," Zoe introduced with enthusiasm.

I greeted each of the girls in turn.

Eve Lambert was tall and thin, with brown eyes and straight brown hair that hung to her shoulders. The youngest of the group at fourteen, she was shy yet polite and always seemed to say all the right things, but her inner light didn't quite reach her eyes. I knew in a minute that Eve was a younger version of myself. Her breeding was too engrained into her personality to allow her to appear bored even though it was obvious she *was* bored. I'm certain she was counting down the minutes until she could retire to her room and dive back into the book she was clutching in one hand.

Prudence "Pepper" Pepperton was a tiny little thing who reminded me a lot of Zoe. She had dark curly hair and blue eyes that danced when she spoke. Pepper was the middle "child" at fifteen. Based on the way she was jumping around with more energy and enthusiasm than could be contained in one body, I was confident in going out on a limb and thinking she was going to be the ice breaker and cheerleader of the group. When I was fifteen I would have found Pepper's enthusiasm exhausting, but now I found myself somewhat enchanted by the elflike girl who ruthlessly abused the English language as she talked a mile a minute about anything and everything.

Blond-haired, blue-eyed Brooklyn Banks was the girl I'd always secretly longed to be. At sixteen she was beautiful and sophisticated, with a natural confidence that stated to the world that she knew what she wanted and knew how to get it. I could never have pulled off the Brooklyn attitude when I was her age, even if I'd been half as beautiful as she. She too looked bored, but unlike Eve, who wanted to dive into a book, I suspected Brooklyn wanted to dive into the boyfriend she'd been forced to leave behind when she'd been kicked out of her last school for smoking in the dorm.

I stepped aside and invited everyone inside as Zoe competed with Pepper for airtime. Zak brought in the luggage as Pepper and Zoe talked a mile a minute, but to be honest, I wouldn't remember a thing either of them said. I smiled as was expected, and I'm sure I was able to string together comprehensible sentences, but I really couldn't remember ever being as nervous as I was at meeting the trio of young women I was about to share my life with.

"Let me show you to your rooms so you can get settled in before dinner," I offered after the luggage had been deposited in my entryway.

Suddenly my house felt full. I hadn't lived with anyone, other than a series of feline companions, since I'd moved out of my parents' house to attend college. I'd had a few opportunities along the way to share my life with a roommate, but I'd always liked the quiet. Not that I hadn't had friends. During my sixty-two years I've shared my life with many wonderful people. But in all that time, I've never shared my life with anyone who was really mine.

Zak and Zoe followed behind the girls as I escorted my new housemates to the rooms I had chosen for them. Each of the three bedrooms I'd selected was large and nicely decorated. Each room had both a bed and sitting area, and each had a private bath.

"I don't do pink," Brooklyn informed me when I opened the door to a bedroom with a pink duvet, pink curtains, and a white sofa.

"I like pink," Pepper offered.

"Very well, then, Pepper, this shall be your room," I decided.

Pepper trotted inside and jumped up on the bed, squealing in delight when she noticed the clawfoot tub in the corner. She hopped off the bed and ran across the room to the tub, which she immediately climbed into to check it out for a comfortable fit.

"Dinner will be at seven. I hope you like pork roast."

"I love all food," Pepper assured me.

I smiled and took a breath. One down, two to go.

Zak delivered Pepper's luggage to her room while Zoe, Brooklyn, and Eve followed me down the hall. I opened the door to the room I had at one time converted into an office and library but had since converted back into a bedroom. The conversion of the room was complete other than the fact that I hadn't had the opportunity to remove all the books from the shelves.

"Bookshelves." Eve gasped. "Lots and lots of bookshelves, packed with all these lovely books. Can this room be mine?"

Brooklyn shrugged. "Fine by me."

Eve walked directly over to the wall that was lined with dark cherry wood shelving. I'd seen the love in her eyes when she'd spotted my rare book collection. I felt some of the tension leave my body, only to return when Eve informed me that she was a vegetarian. I almost panicked until I realized I had both a salad and vegetables to go with the pork roast, as well as whole grain bread I'd picked up that morning from the bakery. My mind immediately turned to other vegetarian options. Perhaps I'd try the new recipe I'd recently found for spinach ravioli lasagna, or maybe even the eggplant casserole I'd recently tried at a friend's house. Two down and only one to go.

The last room was the largest of the three. It was nicely furnished and spacious, but the truly amazing thing about it was the walk-in closet with satin-lined drawers, shoe racks, and a rotating clothing rod. When I noticed Brooklyn's look of boredom turn into one of elation, I knew deep inside that things were going to be all right.

"Do you have any dietary restrictions?" I asked as Brooklyn twirled around in the middle of the huge closet.

"I don't eat carbs."

"No carbs. Got it. Is there anything else I should know?"

Brooklyn stopped twirling and looked at me. "I haven't had a mother for a very long time; I don't need mothering."

"Don't have a mother? But I just recently spoke to your mother."

"I didn't mean literally; I just mean that I'm sixteen and have lived away from home since I was very young. I've attended boarding school during the academic year and camp during the summer since I was six. I'm used to taking care of myself and making my own decisions."

"I see."

Brooklyn must have noticed my look of concern because she quickly followed up with, "Look, I'm not going to be a problem. I promise. It's actually very nice of you to allow me to stay here after I was kicked out of my old school. I just wanted to let you know that I don't need a lot of active parenting."

"All right," I said. "I can respect that, and as long as you follow the house rules and do well in your classes I'll try to give you some space."

"Awesome. I'm going to need to find a local doctor. Can you recommend one?"

"Are you ill?" I asked.

"Birth control."

"Oh." I know I blushed, which I found embarrassing; a woman of my age should be able to discuss birth control without turning red.

God, Phyllis, you are such a child.

After I assured Brooklyn I would get her a list of gynecologists in the area, I left the girls to unpack. Once I'd taken a few deep breaths to steady my pounding heart, I said my good-byes to Zak and Zoe and headed toward the kitchen to check on the meal I'd prepared. I like to cook but rarely do with only myself to feed. It would be nice to have mouths to feed on a regular basis, even if two of them had adopted restricted diets.

I rechecked the oven for what must have been the tenth time that day. The meat looked moist and tender, as I'd hoped it would be. Eve, I decided, was going to miss out on something wonderful.

I put the potatoes on to boil and decided to head into the formal dining room to set the table. I'm not certain why I'd purchased such a large table when I'd bought and furnished the house. I rarely entertained and certainly never fed enough people to even begin to fill each of the twelve hardwood chairs. I planned to set one end of the table to create a more intimate dining experience.

After wiping down the dust-free surface I turned toward the antique hutch I'd bought at an estate sale and considered which place settings to use. This was a special occasion. Perhaps I should use Mama's china. And then again, I didn't want to have the girls feeling awkward by making a fuss. Perhaps the everyday dishes would be fine.

"Can I help?" Pepper asked as she entered the room through the kitchen.

"I'm trying to decide which dishes to use for our dinner."

"Does it matter?"

"No," I admitted. "I suppose it doesn't." I held up two dinner plates. "Which shall it be?"

"The ivory with the small blue flowers."

"There are linens in that drawer behind you. Why don't you pick out some placemats and napkins and I'll fetch the silverware."

Pepper chatted about the food at the last school she'd attended while we worked together to set a beautiful table for our first meal together. When the table was ready she followed me into the kitchen, where she continued to ramble on about various subjects while I prepared the vegetables. Pepper informed me that she too liked to cook, which she proved by preparing a colorful salad while I saw to the beverages. I found I rather liked preparing a meal alongside another person.

"I really love your house," Pepper complimented. "When Mr. Zimmerman pulled up to the front and I saw those blue shutters and all those beautiful flowers I knew I was going to be happy here."

"I'm so glad you like it. I've always liked to garden. Perhaps you'd like to help me when you have some free time."

"I'd like that."

"Tell me about yourself," I urged.

"I'm not sure what there is to tell. My full name is Prudence Partridge Pepperton. It's a mouthful, I know. When I was a baby my nanny began calling me Pepper and it stuck. My father is the only one who ever calls me Prudence."

"And your mom?" I asked.

"She's dead. She committed suicide last winter, after my father left her for one of his creations."

I frowned. "Creations?"

"My father is a plastic surgeon in Beverly Hills."

"I see." Pepper's announcement didn't quite fit with her airy tone of voice. At first I thought she was pulling my leg, but the tension around her eyes said otherwise.

"I am so sorry," I replied. "I really had no idea. That must have been an incredibly difficult time for you."

Pepper shrugged. "Yeah. I guess."

She looked away, struggling, I think, to maintain her composure.

"And why did you decide to attend Zimmerman Academy?" I changed the subject.

"I didn't decide. My father did. He left my mom, and then he didn't want me."

"Oh, I'm sure that isn't true." I couldn't imagine a parent not wanting his child."

"No, it is," Pepper assured me in a very matter-of-fact tone. "When my mom told me that my dad had taken off with one of his creations, I thought there would be a messy custody battle over me, but my father sat me down and told me that he had a new wife and a new life and he thought I'd be better off staying with my mother. I thought he'd visit, but he never did."

I put my hand to my heart to try to keep it from breaking.

"After Mom died I had no choice but to go stay with my father," Pepper continued. "I thought he would be happy to see me, but I could tell I was cramping his style. He knows Mr. Zimmerman somehow, and when he found out about the Academy, he asked if I could attend as a boarder. Mr. Zimmerman said he was thrilled to have me, so here I am."

"Well, I am thrilled to have you as well." I offered her my warmest smile. "I think the five of us are going to have a wonderful time this year."

"Five of us?" Pepper asked.

"You and me, Brooklyn, Eve, and Charlotte."

"Charlotte? I haven't met her."

"Charlotte is my cat. She decided to hide, but I'm sure she'll make an appearance once she gets used to all the commotion."

Pepper smiled. "I always wanted a pet. My father isn't a fan of pet dander, so I was never allowed to have one. Do you think Charlotte would want to sleep with me?"

"Honestly," I replied, "probably not. She's an old cat and set in her ways."

Pepper's smile faded just a bit.

"But perhaps Zoe can find a younger cat for you. She runs a shelter, you know."

Pepper grinned. "Really? A cat of my own?"

"I can't promise that you'll be able to take it with you when you leave here, but as far as I'm concerned the cat can be yours while you're here."

Was I crazy? Charlotte was going to have kittens. Not literally. She was too old for kittens, but I could guarantee she'd throw a diva kitty tantrum.

"Of course you must promise to take care of it," I added. "Having a pet of your own is a big responsibility."

Pepper ran across the room and wrapped her thin arms around my waist. She hugged me harder than I'd ever been hugged, and I felt my heart warm in a way it never had in all the years I'd resided on this planet. I hugged Pepper back and thanked the universe for the momentary insanity that had brought Pepper and the others into my life.

"I'll take care of all her needs. I promise," Pepper assured me.

I smiled. "It's late today, but we can call Zoe tomorrow to see what she has available."

Later that evening I decided to stop in to say good night to Eve. I'd actually managed to discover a fair amount of information about the other two girls, but Eve had been characteristically quiet for most of the evening. I felt that, more than any of the others, I understood Eve. I too was the type to use my words frugally when in a new social situation, but that didn't mean I didn't have anything to say or that I didn't want to feel included.

I knocked on Eve's door. The light was still on, so I knew she was still awake.

"Come in," she called.

I slowly opened the door. Eve was curled up in the big chair near the small wood stove with a book.

"I just wanted to say good night and to make sure you didn't need anything before I retire for the evening."

"Thank you. I'm fine."

I smiled. I really didn't know what else to say, so I began to close the door.

"I love your book collection," she added. "I hope it's okay that I borrowed one."

"Of course." I opened the door wider and stepped inside the room. "Please feel free to read anything you like. I was concerned at first that I should box them up because I was going to have boarders."

"Oh, no. Don't do that. Having a room filled with books is having a room filled with friends."

"I've always felt the same way. Not everyone understands the fact that many of the characters I've grown to love truly feel like people I know. What are you reading this evening?"

"The Perks of Being a Wallflower."

"I haven't read that. Are you enjoying it?"

"I am. I actually just started it, but so far so good. What are you reading?"

Eve and I spent the next thirty minutes talking about my favorite subject: books. Although decades separated us in years, I found we'd read and enjoyed many of the same stories.

"I should be heading to bed," I said with a yawn. "I did want to ask if there was anything you needed, or anything I should know about you other than the fact that you're vegetarian."

Eve looked down at her book, but I could tell that she hadn't gone back to reading. "Not really."

"What made you decide to attend Zimmerman Academy?"

"I didn't decide. Attending the Academy was a deal that my court-appointed shrink and my public defender made with the district attorney to get me out of juvie."

I couldn't have been more shocked if she'd told me she had just arrived from an alien planet. I was beginning to regret my decision not to read the background information Zak had given me on each of the girls more thoroughly until after I met them. I didn't want to have what I read affect my first impressions of them.

"You were in juvie?"

"Yeah. I thought you knew."

"For what?"

"I put my stepdad in the hospital."

"Was it self-defense?" I had to ask.

"Not according to the judge. He said that adding sedatives to the scumbag's whiskey in the hope of rendering him unconscious didn't fall into the category of defending myself. It was the judge's opinion that I should have gone to an adult I trusted rather than taking action on my own. Of course to this point in my life I've never met an adult I trusted enough to share such a big secret."

I frowned. "Did your stepfather abuse you?"

"Every time he drank, and I have the scars to prove it." Eve stopped and looked at me. Her voice softened just a bit. "I didn't mean to actually hurt him; I just wanted to make him pass out. My friend gave me the idea to use the sedatives, so I tracked some down and began adding it to his whiskey. It really seemed to help. Every time he drank he'd fall asleep before he could get nasty. What I didn't know was that the drug I used builds up in your system over time, and he eventually overdosed. He's okay now and back at home, and I know I should feel bad about what I did, but all I actually feel is relieved that my plan succeeded in getting me out of the house."

I found that I was at a loss for words.

"Don't worry. I'm not dangerous," Eve promised me. "I just did a stupid thing."

"I'm not worried," I assured the girl. "I'm glad it worked out for you to come to Ashton Falls. You'll be safe here."

Eve looked down at her book again, but I felt as if we'd made a connection. At least I hoped we had. She, more than the others, seemed to need the kind of environment Zak and I hoped to provide at the Academy.

As I walked toward my room, I had to marvel at the set of circumstances that had landed me as housemother to a sexually active sixteen-year-old, an all-but-orphaned fifteen-year-old, and a fourteen-year-old client of the juvenile justice system.

I entered my room and began my nightly ritual. Charlotte curled up on my pillow as I began removing my makeup and moisturizing my skin. My mother, God rest her soul, had drilled into my head the importance of a proper cleansing and moisturizing ritual when I was still a young woman. She'd taught me a structured routine that I follow to this day.

"I will admit that the day has held its share of surprises," I began as Charlotte watched me go through the predictable steps of the process.

"Still, I have high hopes that the girls and I will do just fine. Pepper talks a mile a minute, so I know none of us will ever have to suffer the agony of awkward silence when she's around," I said aloud, confident that Charlotte actually was listening to my chatter.

"And, although Eve has a tragic past, I'm choosing to leave it in the past. You know, she really is quite interesting, and we like many of the same authors. She's read so many of the classics. I know we'll never lack for books to discuss."

I slipped a flannel nightgown over my head and then began sorting the clothes I had removed. I hung those that could be worn again on hangers and separated those that needed laundering into differing baskets for the laundry service.

"Brooklyn may prove to be a challenge in the long run," I informed Charlotte as I unwound my bun and began brushing my waist-length hair. "We'll have to see how things go. It is a bit odd that she's more experienced with boys and dating than I am. I hope I'll instinctively know how to handle any situations that may arise on that front."

After I brushed my hair one hundred times I fashioned it into a long braid that hung down my back.

"I think all the girls are both nervous and excited to begin classes next week. The transitional school Zak has organized for this year will accommodate ten students, five girls and five boys between the ages of twelve and sixteen, with the exception of Alex, who, as you know is just ten. Three of them will be attending the middle school in the mornings and the other seven will attend the high school. Just the thought of high school fills me with terror, but I think our girls will do just fine."

Charlotte yawned. She appeared to be communicating that she had bored with my chatter. I ignored her.

"I find myself optimistic about the future. We're being offered not only the opportunity to spend more time with people we already love but the chance to bring wonderful new acquaintances into our life as well."

I straightened the bathroom and headed back toward the sleeping area.

"Do you think I should dress up or down for my first day at the Academy?"

"Meow."

"Yes. That's what I thought as well."

After I was satisfied that I had done everything I needed to do to prepare myself for bed, I set to preparing the room. I worked my way around the area, straightening already perfectly straight books and knickknacks before opening my window just a quarter of an inch.

"I'm excited for the meet and greet Zak and Zoe are hosting tomorrow. I think it was such a good idea to provide an informal setting where everyone can get to know one another before classes begin. I would think that having an informal social event before the beginning of the school year will ease first-day jitters for students and staff alike. Of course most of the staff already know one another, but it will be nice to give Mr. Danner, the new teacher of mathematics, a chance to get to know everyone else. He's a widower, you know."

Charlotte tilted her head as she watched me.

"I know what you're thinking, but it's not true. I don't have a crush on Mr. Danner. Yes, he's very good-looking, and we seem to share a lot of interests in common, but he's five years younger than I am. Besides, his wife hasn't been gone all that long. I'm sure the last thing he's interested in doing is dating a sixty-two-year-old virgin."

Charlotte rolled over onto her back. I sat down on the side of the bed and gave her stomach a scratch as I pictured the new math teacher. He did have a nice smile, and the creases in the corners of his eyes turned upward, indicating that he smiled a lot. And really, if you think about it, a five-year age difference wasn't all that insurmountable once you passed the half-century mark.

"I'm just being a silly old woman." I stood up. "A man with Mr. Danner's looks and experience would never be interested in a dried-up old prune like me."

I set my ridiculous fantasies aside and continued with my nightly rituals. After stacking the extra pillows on my white tufted chaise, I poured myself a cup of tea from the warming pot I'd already brought up, and added a splash of brandy. I then slid between my 1500-thread count sheets and settled in.

"Are you ready?"

Charlotte indicated that she was.

After placing my reading glasses on the tip of my nose, I adjusted the light and opened the hardcover book I'd chosen from the bookcase. Charlotte crawled into my lap and began to purr as I began to read aloud. Reading aloud to Charlotte was an activity we both enjoyed immensely, and it was a rare occasion when we missed this ritual at the end of the day. Tonight I'd chosen to once again begin the story of *Emma* by Jane Austin. Emma had spunk. I liked that.

Emma Woodhouse, handsome, clever, and rich, with a comfortable home and happy disposition, seemed to unite some of the best blessings of existence; and had lived nearly twenty-one years in the world with very little to distress or vex her.

I paused and contemplated the sentence. Could a life with little to vex or distress truly be a life worth living? I smiled as I continued with the story. I had a feeling that my controlled and efficient life was about to get a whole lot more complicated, and for the first time I realized that I couldn't wait to see how it all turned out.

Recipes for Heavenly Honeymoon

Recipes by Kathi Daley:

Easy Ice Cream Pie
Easy Lemon Pie
Easy Chocolate Peanut Butter Pie
Apricot Oatmeal Cookies

Recipes by Readers:

Blueberry Catch the Boy Dessert submitted by Joanne Kocourek
Chocolate Cherry Bars submitted by Joyce Aiken
Cooky Candy submitted by Pamela Curran
Rocky Road Pie contributed by Nancy Farris
Poppy Seed Cake submitted by Vivian Shane
Sad Cake submitted by Janel Flynn

Easy Ice Cream Pie

Ingredients:
1 premade graham cracker crust
1 pint any flavor ice cream, softened
8 oz. cream cheese, softened
1 cup confectioner's sugar
1 carton (8 oz.) frozen whipped topping, thawed
1 can pie filling, any flavor
Chocolate or caramel syrup

Layer ice cream into pie crust.
Mix together cream cheese, sugar, and whipped topping.
Layer cream cheese mixture over ice cream.
Add pie filling to top.
Cover and freeze for 3–4 hours.
Drizzle with chocolate or caramel just before serving.

There are a lot of yummy combinations to try. I like chocolate ice cream with cherry or boysenberry topping drizzled with chocolate syrup, or vanilla ice cream with apple filling drizzled with caramel. It's fun to try a variety of combinations.

Easy Lemon Pie

Ingredients:
1 can (14 oz.) sweetened condensed milk
1 can (6 oz.) frozen lemonade concentrate
1 carton (8 oz.) frozen whipped topping, thawed
1 graham cracker crust

Combine milk and lemonade. Fold in whipped topping. Spoon into crust. Chill until ready to serve.

Easy Chocolate Peanut Butter Pie

Ingredients:
1 box graham cracker crust (follow directions on box to make in 9 x 13 pan)
½ cup peanut butter
½ cup chocolate sauce
½ cup corn syrup
3 cups cold milk
1 pkg. instant chocolate pudding
1 carton (12 oz.) frozen whipped topping, thawed
1 cup peanuts, chopped

Mix together peanut butter, chocolate sauce, and corn syrup.
Pour into pie crust.
Whisk milk and pudding for 2 minutes. Let stand 2 minutes.
Spoon into pie crust.
Spread with whipped topping.
Sprinkle with peanuts.
Cover and refrigerate for a couple of hours or until set.

Apricot Oatmeal Cookies

Ingredients:

2 sticks margarine, softened
1½ cups packed brown sugar
⅓ cup molasses
3 eggs
3 cups quick cooking oats
1 tbs. cinnamon
1 tsp. ground nutmeg
1 tsp. ground cloves
1 tsp. baking soda
½ tsp. salt
1 pkg. (6 oz.) dried apricots, chopped

Cream together shortening and brown sugar. Beat in molasses. Add eggs. Mix well. Add dry ingredients. Mix well. Cover and refrigerate 2 hours.

Shape into 1 inch balls. Place 1 inch apart and bake on greased cookie sheet at 350 degrees until browned.

Blueberry Catch the Boy Dessert

Contributed by Joanne Kocourek

My grandma or mom called the cake by the title above. They said it was because the men and boyfriends or brothers would beg for it. It is similar to a blueberry buckle but unique. I added several ingredients that make the cake more to my family members' liking. The original recipe was in one of Grandma's cookbooks from the late 1920s (with Grandma's notations on quantities).

Ingredients:
Cake:

2 cups all-purpose flour, lightly spooned into measuring cup and leveled with a knife
1 tbs. baking powder
1 tsp. salt
2 sticks unsalted butter, softened
¾ cup light brown sugar
½ cup granulated sugar
3 large eggs
1 cup whole buttermilk
1 cup fresh or frozen blueberries (if using frozen berries, thaw, drain well, dry before using)
½ tsp. cinnamon
1 tsp. almond or vanilla extract
¾ tsp. lemon zest

Topping:

1 cup fresh or frozen blueberries
¼ cup light brown sugar
1 tsp. ground cinnamon

Adjust the rack to the best position for baking in your oven and preheat to 350 degrees. Grease and flour a 9 x 13 baking pan and set aside.

Whisk the flour, baking powder, and salt together in a medium bowl. In a large bowl or the bowl of a stand mixer fitted with the paddle attachment, beat the butter, brown sugar, and granulated sugar on medium high speed for about 3 minutes or until light and fluffy (scrape the bowl as necessary).

Add eggs one at a time, beating until just combined after each addition. Reduce speed to medium and add ⅓ of the flour mixture, mixing until incorporated. Mix in ½ cup buttermilk. Repeat with another addition of flour, the rest of the buttermilk, and ending with the final addition of flour. Add the extract and lemon zest. Mix. Gently fold in the blueberries and spread the batter into the prepared pan.

Scatter the additional topping blueberries over the batter. Combine the sugar and cinnamon and sprinkle over the blueberries. Bake for 45–55 minutes or until a toothpick inserted into the center comes out clean. Allow to cool for 20 minutes (or completely) before cutting into squares and serving. Serve warm or at room temperature, plain, topped with sweetened whipped cream, vanilla ice cream, or a simple white icing.

Chocolate Cherry Bars

Submitted by Joyce Aiken

This recipe has been in my recipe box for at least forty years, but we still love it.

Base:

1 pkg. devil's food cake mix
21 oz. can cherry pie filling
1 tsp. almond extract
2 eggs, beaten

Topping:

1 cup sugar
5 tbs. butter or margarine
⅓ cup milk
6 oz. pkg. chocolate chips

Preheat oven to 350 degrees. Grease and flour a 9 x 13 pan. In large bowl, combine the base ingredients and stir by hand until well mixed. Pour into pan and bake 25–30 minutes or until a toothpick inserted near the center comes out clean.

In a small saucepan, combine the sugar, butter, and milk. Bring to a boil, stirring constantly, and stir for one minute after the mixture begins to boil. Remove the pan from the heat and stir in the chocolate chips until chips are smooth. Pour over warm bars. Makes about 3 dozen.

Cooky Candy

Submitted by Pamela Curran

I got this recipe from my mother-in-law, Rose Curran. I make it when I get a chocolate craving. She has passed away, so she would be thrilled for me to share it.

Ingredients:

1 stick margarine
2 cups sugar
⅓ cup cocoa
½ cup milk

Bring to a rolling boil for 1 minute or so. Remove from heat and add:

3 cups quick cooking oats
½ cup of nuts (pecans are preferable)
½ cup coconut
1 tsp. vanilla

Mix together and drop by teaspoon on wax paper. Let cool until firm.

These also freeze well. The serving amount depends on how big you make the cookies.

Rocky Road Pie

Contributed by Nancy Farris

One of our favorite desserts for hot summer days! Did I mention how easy it is?

1 graham cracker crust
1 qt. chocolate ice cream, softened
½ cup peanuts, coarsely chopped
¼ cup chocolate chips
½ cup marshmallow cream
¼ cup chocolate syrup, split

Combine ice cream, peanuts and chocolate chips until well mixed. Put in crust. Swirl in the marshmallow cream and 2 tbs. of the chocolate syrup for a marbled effect. Top with the remaining chocolate syrup and top with additional chopped peanuts. Freeze for at least 2 hours until firm. Cut into slices, top with whipped cream if desired, and enjoy!

Poppy Seed Cake

Submitted by Vivian Shane

This simple cake is one of my favorites because it doesn't need frosting!

1 box yellow cake mix (without pudding)
3 tbs. poppy seeds
1 small pkg. vanilla instant pudding
½ tsp. baking powder
¾ cup Wesson oil, butter flavor (add ½ tsp. butter flavor if not buttery oil)
4 eggs
1 cup hot water
1 tsp. vanilla extract

Mix all ingredients together.
Pour batter into greased and floured Bundt pan.
Bake at 350 degrees for 40 minutes. Cool and remove from pan.

Optional: sprinkle with powdered sugar.

Sad Cake

Submitted by Janel Flynn

This recipe was one my Great-Aunt Mary Etta Branum liked to make.

4 eggs
1 box brown sugar
¾ cup oil
2 cups Bisquick
1 cup coconut
1 cup pecans
2 tsp. vanilla

Mix together in order given. Mix by hand. Bake in a 9 x 13 pan greased and floured at 350 degrees for 30 minutes.

I've used walnuts instead of pecans and it tastes just as good. Quick and easy recipe for summer.

Books by Kathi Daley

Come for the murder, stay for the romance.
Buy them on Amazon today.

Zoe Donovan Cozy Mystery:

Halloween Hijinks
The Trouble With Turkeys
Christmas Crazy
Cupid's Curse
Big Bunny Bump-off
Beach Blanket Barbie
Maui Madness
Derby Divas
Haunted Hamlet
Turkeys, Tuxes, and Tabbies
Christmas Cozy
Alaskan Alliance
Matrimony Meltdown
Soul Surrender
Heavenly Honeymoon
Hopscotch Homicide – *August 2015*
Ghostly Graveyard – *October 2015*
Santa Sleuth – *December 2015*

Paradise Lake Cozy Mystery:

Pumpkins in Paradise
Snowmen in Paradise
Bikinis in Paradise
Christmas in Paradise
Puppies in Paradise
Halloween in Paradise – *August 2015*

Whales and Tails Cozy Mystery:

Romeow and Juliet
The Mad Catter
Grimm's Furry Tail
Much Ado About Felines – *July 2015*
Legend of Tabby Hollow – *September 2015*
Cat of Christmas Past – *November 2015*

Seacliff High Mystery:

The Secret
The Curse
The Relic – *July 2015*
The Conspiracy – *October 2015*

Road to Christmas Romance:

Road to Christmas Past

Kathi Daley lives with her husband, kids, grandkids, and Bernese mountain dogs in beautiful Lake Tahoe. When she isn't writing, she likes to read (preferably at the beach or by the fire), cook (preferably something with chocolate or cheese), and garden (planting and planning, not weeding). She also enjoys spending time on the water when she's not hiking, biking, or snowshoeing the miles of desolate trails surrounding her home.

Kathi uses the mountain setting in which she lives, along with the animals (wild and domestic) that share her home, as inspiration for her cozy mysteries.

Stay up-to-date with her newsletter, *The Daley Weekly*. There's a link to sign up on both her Facebook page and her website, or you can access the sign-in sheet at: http://eepurl.com/NRPDf

Visit Kathi:
Facebook at Kathi Daley Books,
www.facebook.com/kathidaleybooks

Kathi Daley Teen –
www.facebook.com/kathidaleyteen

Kathi Daley Books Group Page –
https://www.facebook.com/groups/5695788231468 50/

Kathi Daley Books Birthday Club- get a book on your birthday - https://www.facebook.com/groups/1040638412628912/

Kathi Daley Recipe Exchange - https://www.facebook.com/groups/752806778126428/

Webpage - www.kathidaley.com

E-mail - kathidaley@kathidaley.com

Recipe Submission E-mail – kathidaleyrecipes@kathidaley.com

Goodreads: https://www.goodreads.com/author/show/7278377.Kathi_Daley

Twitter at Kathi Daley@kathidaley - https://twitter.com/kathidaley

Tumblr - http://kathidaleybooks.tumblr.com/

Amazon Author Page - http://www.amazon.com/Kathi-Daley/e/B00F3BOX4K/ref=sr_tc_2_0?qid=1418237358&sr=8-2-ent

Pinterest - http://www.pinterest.com/kathidaley/

Made in the USA
San Bernardino, CA
10 July 2019